DWIDALA CAMERA SHOP

AJIT NATHANIEL

Vitasta

Published by
Renu Kaul Verma
Vitasta Publishing Pvt Ltd
4348/4C, Ansari Road, Daryaganj
New Delhi - 110002
info@vitastapublishing.com

ISBN: 978-81-988295-6-6

First Edition 2025

MRP ₹ 399

Layout by Shubhpreet Kaur
Cover Design by Deepanshu Tyagi
Printed by Vikas Computer and Printers, New Delhi

Contents

Dedicated To

Vivien—my light, my life—seeing the world through your eyes has been the greatest joy. Your observations and pronouncements have been entertaining and enlightening, and have nudged me along on my own spiritual journey.

And

Chloe Maya—my first ever teacher of the true power of mindfulness and presence.

Small Small Baby Puppy:
She's giving a flick.

Big Big Papa Dog: No Vivi,
that's the Buddha, and he's
doing the Chin Mudra with
his right hand.

Small Small Baby Puppy:
No. She's giving a flick.

Big Big Papa Dog: Yes Vivi,
she's giving a flick—to
Samsara.

Chapter 1

Tripadvisor reviews are nonsense.

The Baxterpur monastery and the resident meditation programme are completely overrated. Now I'm not some wannabe meditator who found six hours of silent meditation too much for my monkey mind to handle. No—I've done a couple of meditation workshops since the divorce, so I get it—but Lama Phuntsok—is to Dhyana what the Instagram Yogini is to Ashtanga. Three hours of talking in circles—spouting literal gibberish on soul, presence, mind and body, and seven chakras—fawned upon by six starstruck Delhi socialites. Then the meditation—three hours of sitting in lotus position with his gibberish continuing in a throaty monotone. No chance of meditating at all.

Baxterpur is a peculiar place—that's nestled in the hills of Uttarakhand with a line of sight to both Tibet and Nepal. It's a picturesque town named after a British military officer, located along a mountain road that connects nowhere to nowhere. Baxterpur has all the trappings of these mountain towns—a church built by Scottish Presbyterians in 1875, four summer palaces once owned by Northern Indian Maharajas—now hoity-toity guesthouses—and a number of Victorian cottages also operating as posh guesthouses.

Tripadvisor was right about one thing though—Baxterpur is beautiful. As far as the eyes can see, pale green hills glow under the March sun, punctuated by the last patches of snow that will melt away in a day or two. Baxter Lodge where I am staying is a pricey inn with twelve rooms—eight within the imposing two-storey Baxter House—and four in the former servant quarters. My room in the latter is comfortable and I prefer it to the ones in the house. It has a veranda out front where I can sit and read.

Unfortunately, like all picturesque places on Trip Advisor, Baxterpur is crawling with photographers—well, not exactly crawling with them, but every other person carries a camera. All the guests at Baxter Lodge have cameras. Oh, and there are Social Media Influenzas making Instagram reels at every hairpin turn—sometimes even holding up traffic while recording in the centre of the road.

Since I'd paid for a fortnight, I thought I'd just make the best of it and get some photographs.

I decided not to return to the meditation programme.

For a serious photographer, the choice of lens for a walk is torturous. My Fujifilm camera has a great all-purpose lens for walking around—I've got some of my best shots on it. But I also love my expensive portrait lens for those super-sharp portraits that make the subject pop out of a blurry background. It's a pain to switch lenses on the fly—dust could land on the sensor, or one could drop a lens—like I did in Pushkar. Here in Baxterpur, I needed both lenses—the walkabout lens to capture the amazing landscapes—and the portrait lens perfect for the photogenic, sunburnt monks—who pop up in all Baxterpur Instagram posts. The decision was too difficult—I just took the entire bag of gear.

I walked down the path from Baxter Lodge. I managed a few unremarkable pictures of the breathtaking valley—decided to just tramp around until evening came—and the light softened.

Dwidala Camera Shop.

Dwidala—Ajna Pankaja—Lama Phuntsok had seven terms for the Third Eye Chakra, during his drawn-out monologues. How cliche—a camera shop named after the mythical third eye chakra in a monastery town. Curiously, no boards proclaiming Nikon, Canon, or Sony—the holy trinity of digital photography—just the shop's name in the Tibetan style font that makes English look like Hebrew. The shop's exterior was painted in the deep vermillion shade of a Tibetan monk's cloak.

Not having much else to do, I decided to enter.

The shop's interior was painted in the same deep red. A long glass counter displayed a variety of old cameras. Behind the display was a bright red storage unit with square eight-inch compartments running the entire length of the shop. It had gold hinges and shiny ivory knobs. At the far end, was a square window, covered by an orange-gold shutter.

'Hello.'

I was startled by a voice from somewhere in the shadows. At the far end of the counter, hunched over a tiny lamp and a magnifying glass, was a portly, bald monk in customary attire.

'Uh hello,' I responded.

As my eyes were adjusting to the low light of the shop, I was amused by the weirdness of it all—a camera shop without all the bright lights and displays—just those crappy old film cameras and unknown mysteries in those red boxes.

The monk turned back to a tiny device under the lamp. He purposefully placed the magnifying glass on the counter and made a barely discernible adjustment with a micro screwdriver. He picked up the magnifying glass for another look and then put it back on the table. He switched off the light and walked towards me.

'What do you shoot?' he asked.

'Fuji. XT3.'

The monk stepped into the light. I was amused—he was a life-sized replica of the laughing Buddha—bald, fat, stubby-nosed, with deep laugh lines.

'Anything I can do for you?' he asked.

'I'm just looking around, but can you do a sensor cleaning?'

'Let me take a look.'

I handed him the camera with the walkabout lens attached. He took it from me gently and turned it around in his hands—examining it in the daylight that shone through the window.

'How was Pushkar this time?'

'It was fine fi…wait—how did you know that I've been in Pushkar?'

'The sand. It gets everywhere.'

He switched on the camera, pointed it out the window, spun the aperture dial and clicked. His movements were gentle, precise, and purposeful. No sense of exaggeration or flair. No hesitation.

'So how was Pushkar?'

'Same as every year—more tourists, fewer camels, more of a mess.'

I liked the monk. For the first time since I bought this expensive camera, I had met someone who treated it gentler than I do. I remembered that cretin at a shop in Delhi, who placed the camera sensor side up on the counter, and then blew into it before putting a lens back on. When I protested, he laughed at me. 'This is the only camera you have—but I handle a hundred such cameras every day. I know how they should be treated'. Bastard.

The monk took the camera to the corner of the shop where the light on the counter was. He reached under the counter and pulled out a Tupperware box full of odds and ends. Opening it, he took out two sensor swabs, a brush, a blower, a bottle of cleaning fluid, and a few cleaning wipes. I wanted to ask him the cost of the sensor cleaning, but my experience thus far had been positive—I just didn't want to interrupt the dance of his hands.

I watched as he methodically used the air blower, then put the lens on and checked the camera—then used the brush and checked the camera again. Then the swab. He checked the camera again. It was a pleasure to watch him at work—unhurried, meticulous, completely engrossed. He walked up to the window and took a few pictures—he looked at the pictures through the viewfinder and on the camera's LCD screen. With his face gleaming with almost smug satisfaction, he set the camera on the counter with the lens facing me.

'Check it.'

'You seem to have done a thorough job—I'm sure it is alright.'

'What is alright for me may not be alright for you. Check it.'

OK, so maybe spouting this Zen gobbledygook

comes with the monk costume.

I took the camera to the door and took some pictures of the sky at f/22 aperture. No sensor spots. So, what was alright for the monk was alright for me after all.

I walked back into the shop—scanning the display cases for something that I could buy. Nothing but film cameras—good condition—pity that I don't have the patience to shoot film.

'How much will it be for the cleaning?'

'Cleaning and inspection are complimentary.'

'Sorry?'

'No charge.'

I didn't know what to say. Hardly anyone in Delhi wet-cleans a sensor. Even the Fujifilm people charge a bomb to do it. The smaller shops do it with a million caveats, insisting that they will not be responsible for any damage to the sensor and so forth.

'Anything else I can do for you?"

I scanned the display a little more carefully—and no, nothing that I could possibly buy from him.

'I don't think so.'

'Have you had lunch?'

'Er, lunch? No, not yet.'

'OK—join me,' he offered.

'Er, actually...'

'No, I insist. It's time for lunch. Enjoy some nice Tibetan food.'

He rapped the golden shutter with his knuckles and motioned to a low table with two stools in the far corner of the shop.

Just as we were seated, a Tibetan boy walked into the shop with a heavy tray balanced on his shoulder. He put down two small bowls of noodle soup, two plates of stir-fried meat, and a plate with four of those soggy bun things that you get at Tibetan eating places. He placed a tall glass of water before the monk, and in front of me—a bottle of Canada Dry.

I froze—staring blankly as he popped off the cap in a snappy manoeuvre using his steel bangle.

Canada Dry. I didn't know they still made it. Was this the imported one?

No—it had the same markings that I remembered from childhood—who sells these drinks in glass bottles anymore?

Canada Dry.

It was around when I was in school. I was never keen on colas—something about Canada Dry appealed to me—I don't know—maybe it was the exclusivity of demanding a beverage at an eating joint and be told—sorry we only have Coca Cola and Thums Up—and then respond, 'OK, then just a glass of water for me'.

Or maybe not—I was quite the simpleton in school. Maybe, I just liked the fresh, unusual taste. It disappeared from the market around the time I finished high school, and I've never tasted it since.

I took a sip of the crisp, effervescent beverage—maybe it was the shock of the icy cold liquid in my mouth or the sugar hitting my bloodstream—but, what just happened?

Barely 30 seconds had elapsed since the monk had knocked on the shutter—a minute at the most. And here we were already, with a piping hot meal for two and a soft drink that had time travelled from the 1990s. What was this—a setup? Was this one of those gangs that drug you and rob you? Was I going to wake up at the bottom of the valley minus my camera kit and kidneys? The monk must know that he can't get away with it—cell phones are tracked, people see things.

The monk looked me in the eye. 'One problem with Samsara is that its omnipresent, unsubstantial anxiety can poison even the tiniest opportunity for joy.'

Great. So, I'm stuck with a chubby Lama Phuntsok for the price of a sensor cleaning.

The monk had a point though. I took a deep breath of the steam from the soup. It smelt delicious. I took a couple of sips. The monk was eating everything at the same time—a spoon of the soup, a bite of the bread with the meat—I wondered if the salad-soup-entree-dessert protocol was just an occidental effort to add some meaning and structure to Samsara. I also wondered why I was beginning to think so deeply.

'So how does a monk end up selling cameras?'

'Cameras are tools of consciousness and perception.

We blow through the world at the speed of life. Sometimes we take pictures. What happens when you look at a picture you took some time ago?'

I shrugged, 'It takes you back, I suppose.'

'To what?'

'The moment. The place. The feelings.'

'Yes. You remember—not just the moment, but the moments before, the moments after, the things people said, the things you wish you said, the emotions you felt...'

'True,' I agreed.

'Cameras are an anchor to your past.'

'But why film cameras?' I asked.

'Because digital cameras don't work that way.'

'What?' I looked puzzled.

'How many pictures have you taken with your Fuji?'

'About 20,000.'

'How many digital pictures have you taken in your life?'

'Maybe 50,000 including shots from my phone and my pocket camera.'

The number seemed enormous.

'How many have you gone back to look at?'

'Maybe 200. And that too, not too often.'

'Those pictures are mostly for social media—correct?'

'Yes.'

'So, with the film camera, you get 36 shots per roll—each shot costs money. You can't immediately see what the shot looks like, so you need to be technically proficient. You need to be good with how you expose—the right lighting, composition, and focus. Like meditation, you need to work on your skills with all of these—and then you get the ability to capture those images and collect your keys to memories.'

'Except for the limitations with the roll, there's no real difference from digital cameras?' I asked.

'There is! You '*freeze*' that moment by trapping light chemically on your film. In a darkroom, you again use light and chemicals to put it on paper. At the end of your process, you get your memory on a paper card—something you can physically hold in your hand, put in an album, hang on a wall or send by post. When you share it with someone, you're sending them a thing—solid, tangible matter—or you sit with them side-by-side and talk to them, drawing them into the moment.'

The monk stopped talking and turned his attention back to his plate. I started eating too and it wasn't until I was almost done with my first bun that the meaning of what he had said began to emerge.

'*Stay in the moment,*' the monk said. 'Enjoy your food—you won't find Shabtra like this once you leave Baxterpur.'

The food was delicious. I had eaten at many places in the Tibetan neighbourhood in New Delhi, the Shabtra, and this bun thing, but I never remember it being as good as this. But again, I never went to Majnu Ka Tila purely for the food. I mostly dined there with the artsy women I met on Tinder and OKCupid; the alcohol-free, inexpensive, cramped eating joints in a colourful and stimulating neighbourhood were a setup for other intentions, but I digress.

The monk finished his meal a few minutes before I did. He turned sideways, pushed his stool against the wall, and sat back. That was really kind of him, because it sort of eased the awkwardness of this unexpected meal with a stranger.

I finished my meal and continued to nurse what was left of the Canada Dry.

'Your theory of cameras being anchors to the past is interesting.'

'Did you enjoy your meal?'

'Yes, very much—I've eaten Tibetan food before, but you're right—I've never tasted Shabtra this good.'

'This shop is dark. Your iris is probably at its widest opening—equivalent to about f/2.8 on a camera. At a film speed of 800, that's a shutter-speed of 1/50th of a second. This means that every second of the time that you spend here is 50 slices of experience in your consciousness—each slice of experience comprises sight, smell, touch, sound, thought, emotion. If you had a memory card trying to store just those images, you would be using a 64 GB card for every minute of your life.'

'That's an interesting perspective. So how do I turn my

Fuji camera into an anchor to my past?'

'What lenses do you have?'

'Most of them—the 18-55 of course, primes—the 35/1.4, the 56/1.2 and the 90/2.'

'Primes mostly.'

'Yes.'

'You're halfway there. You could consider a manual lens. Not having autofocus will slow you down a bit—it will make you think a little bit about your shot. It's nothing like film, but it should get you to think of your photos as slices of consciousness.'

Ah, the sale.

'Do you have a lens I could use?'

The monk stood up and walked to the storage case. He opened a compartment with a single lens in it, retrieved it and gently placed it on the counter. From another compartment, he retrieved a metal ring about two inches in diameter.

'Helios 44 and an adapter to use it on your camera.'

'How much?'

'Is there anything in the bag that you would want to let go? I do very favourable exchanges.'

'Not really—I need all the lenses I own.'

'Are you using them all?' he asked.

'I guess so, but wait, I have an old Canon pocket digital—eight years old, a bit beaten up, but I don't use it much anymore.'

'Let me have a look.'

I extracted the camera, its two spare batteries, and charger from the side pocket of my bag. The monk examined them, turning the camera on and off.

'Old, but working. This is a fair trade.'

'Really?' I was incredulous.

'Yes.'

I put the lens and the camera in my bag.

'Thank you so much for the sensor cleaning, the lens, and the tasty lunch.'

'Thank you for the company over lunch.' The monk gave me a warm parting smile.

I left the shop feeling somewhat disoriented. I think my mind was struggling with what had just happened. Before I knew it, I was halfway back to Baxter Lodge. I noticed something odd—it looked as if the sun had hardly moved since I had set out. The shadows of the trees looked the same.

I walked into the lobby of Baxter Hall and it felt as if I had just left. This couldn't be—between the sensor cleaning, the lunch, and the trip to and from Dwidala Camera Shop I expected at least an hour and a half to have passed. I sat at the coffee bar in the lobby to get my thoughts together. Chaaya—the 'guest manager' flashed me her 1,000-watt smile and asked me if I would like some coffee. I asked her for a cappuccino and watched as she worked the mammoth coffee machine across the room.

Each moment a slice of experience in consciousness.

Each slice a photograph, with emotion, senses, perceptions attached.

Stay In the Moment.

I smelt the rich coffee powder as Chaaya ground the seeds. The rhythmic tapping as she settled the coffee powder in the portafilter. The gentle tinkle as she placed the tamper back on a porcelain plate. The hiss of the machine as she drew a shot; the smell of the coffee growing stronger, then the gushing of the milk frother as she foamed the milk.

Click, click, click—60 MB image files filling up an SD card. Emotion, perception, opinion: hissing upward into some ethereal cloud storage.

She placed the coffee in front of me.

'Mr Arya, are you alright?'

'I think so—It's just…'

The cup of coffee came up towards me—the smell of the coffee—image files loading up the memory card.

'Mr Arya!' I heard her shriek through what seemed like a fog—I felt her hand on my shoulder—her other hand steadying my face.

'Kishan! Roop Singh! Bhishambar!'

Chapter 2

I woke up in an unfamiliar room.

Bhishambar, the Baxter Lodge gardener, was sitting on the floor at the foot of the bed.

Seeing me awake, he stood up and left.

Chaaya entered a few moments later.

'Mr Arya, how're you feeling?'

'I'm alright—just a little light headed I think. What happened?'

'You fainted in the lobby. Doctor Bhatnagar is on his way here, please rest for a bit.'

'I'm alright, really.'

'Please, just until the doctor gets here.'

'OK,' I said feebly.

Doctor Bhatnagar arrived ten minutes later—the typical English countryside physician, right out of a 1900s novel. He was an older man—mid-seventies perhaps—tall, with a shock of white hair, pink skin with sunburnt cheeks, and a brown doctor's valise.

He opened up his bag and pulled out a stethoscope.

'Arya, right?'

'Yes doctor, Harish Arya.'

He checked my pulse, peered under my eyelids, looked at my fingernails, and examined my fingertips.

'What kind of work do you do?'

'Nothing really—I ran a small company until I sold it two years ago—I'm just riding out some contractual terms that prevent me from starting another business for a while.'

'Right. Was your working life particularly busy?'

'Yes—twelve to twenty hours a day, eight days a week.'

'Are you on any kind of a fad diet?'

'Sorry?'

'One of these stupid diets where you eat only meat or only fruits, or only drink juice or some such nonsense?'

'No—in fact I just enjoyed a nice Tibetan meal with soup, Shaptra, and steamed buns.'

'Right.' The doctor paused for a moment and the hint of a smile appeared on his lips. 'Nothing wrong here—just your mind decompressing.'

'What?'

'Your mind can't handle the peace here—when you work for years in a high stress environment you lose the ability to handle calm. No matter what you try, nothing stressful can happen here in Baxterpur, so your brain just kicked itself on the shin and shut down. Also, we're about eight thousand feet above sea level, so the air is thinner. Lesser oxygen.'

'How long are you here for?'

'Another couple of weeks at least, maybe more.'

'OK. Try to relax.'

'That's it? No medicine or any other tips?'

'Do you drink alcohol Arya?'

'Sometimes.'

'OK,' he drew a spiral pad and a slim steel ballpoint pen from his pocket. 'I prescribe one, just one, large scotch to be taken at the western Gazebo every evening at sunset.' He scribbled something on the pad.

'I'll leave the prescription with Chaaya.'

'Unusual prescription, but okay. You seem to be quite familiar with this.'

'Oh, I spent forty years in the army. Something like this happens to every paratrooper after retirement. Maroons go bloody bonkers unless they're jumping out of planes and having mortar rounds fired at them a few times a day. Here in Baxterpur this happens to a lot of you IT types.'

He packed his stethoscope and left.

Chaaya entered the room.

'I have your prescription, Mr Arya.' She giggled, waving a slip of paper.

'Could you please call me Harish? Mr Arya sounds really odd.'

'Alright.'

'May I have that cup of coffee?'

'Sure thing. Also, your camera bag is safe with me. I'll send it to your room.'

I returned to the lobby and waited for Chaaya to bring me my coffee. I could feel her touch on my shoulder and face, where she had touched me—getting warmer as she drew closer. I felt the pressure from all the data my mind was processing—the pressure from my arousal—the coffee smell, and the other fruity, flowery notes from the mysterious smells that hang over women—cherry lip balm, tea tree shampoo, Guerlain Shalimar.

Yes, Guerlain Shalimar no doubt about it.

For this twenty-something working in customer service at a mountain inn, wearing an obscure classic fragrance was something unusual. But then, there were other unusual things about her too—the sincere smile—not the forced sneer of the Etihad Airways Boarding Pass Ladies.

The perfect cappuccino perfectly centred on a circular serviette on a porcelain saucer, with a spotless teaspoon and two sachets of demerara sugar.

The next slice of experience took in the fir-shaped pattern Chaaya made on my coffee. This wasn't the first time I was seeing it of course—every morning at breakfast I'd sip this coffee while mindlessly scrolling through my phone. The froth of the coffee gave it texture—like the megapixels people demand on digital cameras—that add more detail to the images they produce—like an albino deodar tree lying in a bed of sand.

I didn't add sugar to my coffee and sipped it with intention. I remember reading a flyer near the coffee machine that spoke about this coffee coming from an ancient strain brought from North Africa to the hills of Southern India by an ascetic. Perhaps it was just me being attentive, or maybe it was the memory of that origin story—the coffee tasted rich—beyond the cardinal taste of mud that all coffee has. I detected hints of chocolate, black currant, vanilla. I'd done so many of these mindfulness and meditation workshops since the divorce, I wondered why I never experienced the clarity that I felt in that moment.

I took an hour to finish my cup of coffee. The last drops were cold with ridges of dried foam holding them from me.

The camera bag was in my room when I returned to it.

I took out the Helios lens and adapter to take a good look at them. Both looked brand new—absolutely spotless. I got online and looked the lens up. The Helios 44 is a variant of a German lens designed in 1939. The Russians ransacked the Carl Zeiss factory in Germany after the Third Reich fell. They took Zeiss's optical designs back to the USSR and manufactured these lenses in a factory in the Ukraine. Digging deeper, I discovered that the lens I had was a rare early edition—crusty and battered versions were listed on eBay for a hundred dollars. This one—apparently unused for 60 years and absolutely spotless—must be priceless. I had got this one in exchange for a digital camera that I had bought eight years ago. Something was really up with that monk.

I turned my attention back to the lens. When I unscrewed the rear cap, I noticed a tiny gold lotus bud embossed into the metal. The adapter too had an identical motif. I spent the next few hours playing around with my new lens and looking at 500px for the pictures that other Fujifilm users had taken with it.

The next day, I went for a walk on the hill behind Baxter Lodge. I took my camera and just the Helios lens to see what kind of pictures I'd get with it. Within an hour I was quite pleased. The lens lacked the clinical sharpness of the Fujifilm lenses, and rendered blurred backgrounds with a hypnotic swirl. It was a great lens.

About a kilometre up from the lodge, I noticed a human figure lying prone on a flat patch of grass by the side of the road. It was a woman in denim dungarees and a straw hat hunched over a camera. I was a bit annoyed—it felt like an intrusion—but again, these hills weren't really private property. While I was still wondering if I should introduce myself, she turned to look at me.

Chaaya. My annoyance evaporated.

'Good morning, Harish!' She got to her feet. 'How're you feeling today?'

'I'm fine thanks.' Despite swapping her modest but flattering grey uniform dress for this Tom Sawyer outfit, she was still as attractive.

'I'm feeling much better. I'm so sorry for yesterday—I hope I wasn't too much trouble.'

'Oh, don't worry about it—I'm glad it was nothing serious—just make sure you take the medicine that Dr Bhatnagar prescribed!' She laughed.

'Not at the Lodge today?'

'No, it's my afternoon off. These few days are a good opportunity to get some pictures of insects and plants coming back after the snow, so I'm out taking some shots.'

'Oh nice! Can I see some pictures?'

She pursed her lips and shrugged apologetically. 'Sorry, can't right now.' She held up her camera. 'Film.'

'You shoot film?'

She shrugged.

'Fantastic! You know what, let me not keep you now. I'll catch you at your coffee break one of these days and you can tell me all about shooting film.'

She didn't reply—she just smiled.

'Talk soon!'

'Bye.' She waved hesitantly.

I sat up at night editing the images that I shot that day. The monk was right. I had taken only a dozen pictures over the three hours that I had been outdoors. With any of my Fuji lenses, it would have been over a hundred.

The next day, when I was returning to my room from breakfast, I heard Chaaya call my name. I turned around—she was just a few steps behind me standing with her weight on one foot, wringing her hands.

'Hi,' I said, surprised.

'Hi, I just wanted to say—I hope you didn't think of me as rude or arrogant yesterday. The Baxter Lodge has a strict policy against socialising with guests. I'd love to talk with you about my photography sometime, but it can't happen while you're staying here.'

'I understand. Thanks for letting me know.'

That evening, she brought me my scotch in the Western Gazebo with a subtle smile—perhaps in silent acknowledgement of an inside joke. Nothing seemed different, or she was working really hard to make it seem that way. As I watched her walk back towards the main building, I realised that since the time I had come to Baxter Lodge, Chaaya had been the highlight of my stay. Watching her arrive and depart—with my coffee, scotch, peach preserve, had given me more joy than anything else in this place.

I wanted that coffee with her.

Finding another place in Baxterpur was easier than I imagined. Hillcrest Cottage was a short distance from Baxter Lodge—a three-bedroom property overlooking the valley—no Western gazebo, no coffee shop, no bar, but it had a live-in caretaker-cook. The travel agent in New Delhi who helped me book this place highlighted that the caretaker could get me *maal*—the Delhi word for

Hashish. I paid immediately to rent the place for a month. I asked about alcohol, and the agent said he would send me the bottles I wanted against advance payment.

When I checked out of the Baxter Lodge, Chaaya brought me my bill in the lobby.

'Would you like a cup of coffee before you leave?' she asked.

'Yes please. I'd really like that.'

When she brought me the coffee, I looked up at her. 'I'm moving to Hillcrest cottage.' I wrote my cell-phone number on the circular serviette. 'Perhaps on one of your afternoons off we could have a cup of coffee and you could tell me about your photography.'

She smiled at me—her gaze lingering longer than usual, took the serviette, and walked away.

Hillcrest cottage was nice—not as indulgent as Baxter Lodge, but good. Som, Hillcrest's caretaker was a great cook—serving up chicken, mutton, and buffalo in spicy curries at lunch and dinner. He even baked bread in a makeshift oven built with bricks and an ancient iron cauldron. True to his word, the agent sent up a stock of scotch, vodka, gin, and red wine—everything that I had asked for.

I bitterly missed seeing Chaaya though. I did walk up the hill behind Baxter Lodge once, but I didn't see her there.

Three days after I left Baxter Lodge, I received a text message from an unfamiliar number.

Hi Harish, Chaaya here. How's it going? Are you still in Baxterpur?

Hi Chaaya, yes, I'm still at Hillcrest.

How're you liking it there?

It's alright. It's not as great as Baxter Lodge of course. I miss the coffee, the peach preserve, and of course the staff.

I have the morning off tomorrow. Can I join you at Hillcrest for breakfast?

Of course. What time?

Eight?

Done.

I told Som that I was expecting a guest for breakfast and asked him to have some fresh bread ready.

At 8 am sharp the next morning, Chaaya walked through the gate at Hillcrest Cottage.

I greeted her at the front door and there was that moment of awkwardness when we weren't sure if we should hug. She held a large book flat against her chest, so that was the end of that. I ushered her towards the back garden where Som had laid out breakfast.

As soon as Som saw her, his body language changed. His manner became formal, controlled—extra polite. It seemed as if he was using the opportunity to pitch for a job at the Baxter Lodge.

Breakfast was eggs to order, fresh bread with store bought butter and jam, and coffee. With a conspiratorial smile, Chaaya produced a glass bottle from her bag—the Baxter Lodge peach preserve.

'Thank you so much for coming. I was really looking forward to seeing you again. And thanks for the preserve—I'll be honest, when I say that life isn't the same without it.'

'I had to. I admire your sense of decency. I've just had no end of trouble with male guests at the Baxter Lodge.'

'I can imagine.'

'So did you really want to talk about photography?'

'Yes.'

Som brought scrambled eggs for me.

She put the large book on a vacant chair by the table. 'These are my pictures. We can look at them together after we eat.'

'I'd like that very much. But tell me—why film?'

'I don't know. Perhaps I like the suspense. The feeling of not knowing whether my photos will be alright. There's also the sense of making something tangible—something physical.' She pointed to the big book she had brought. 'I've been taking pictures since the first iPhone came out. I probably have 50,000—maybe more—pictures sitting on hard drives. Some great pictures—London, Switzerland, Bali, Santorini, Maldives, Seychelles, Lake Cuomo, the Azure Coast… but for some reason I never get back to them.'

'Makes sense. I shoot digital too—I feel the same way.'

'How long have you been shooting?'

'Well, I've only had a camera for a few years. I have a Fuji now. I just got my first manual lens a few days ago, and have been thinking of getting into film,' I said.

'Oh, so you've been to Dwidala Camera Shop.'

'Yes. So, you know him too?'

'Haha! Yes, that's where I got my camera from.'

'What's his deal? Is he really a monk?'

'Well, I think he is a monk—very perceptive, very deep, comfortable to talk to. I think he enjoys his Shabtra and dislikes eating alone.'

Som brought Chaaya's omelette.

She reached into her bag and fished out a bottle of dark powder. 'Make our coffee with this please, Som.' She held the bottle out to him.

'*Ji* madam,' Som said quietly and took the bottle from her.

'You know him?'

'Yes!' Chaaya laughed. 'It's part of my job to know all the service staff in the cottages here. Baxterpur is a small place—everyone wants to work at the Baxter Lodge. Som is great. He's a trained cook—he used to work for a Frenchman who lived in Brodie House—just up the road. He learnt to bake bread, madeleines, and make all kinds of continental desserts. This house is owned by a billionaire from Delhi—despite what Som is worth, I can't match what he's being paid now. Also, there's his hashish habit that could be a problem in the consistent and structured experience that we're trying to create at the Lodge.'

'Ah, so how does the Baxter Lodge feel about you pilfering coffee and peach preserve to feed guests who deserted the property for cheaper digs?'

'They won't know if you don't tell!'

We finished our food and Som brought the coffee. Chaaya picked up the photo album and pulled her chair beside mine. There it was again—cherry tree lip balm, tea tree shampoo, Guerlain Shalimar. I fought to stay in the moment with my slices of experience.

The photo album was unique. Instead of the albums that have four or six small pictures per page, Chaaya's album had just one large photo on each leaf. Big, bold prints. She shot colour film—something with vivid greens.

There were pictures of grasshoppers, tiny birds, blades of grass with dew on them, a baby lizard—all captured in rich colour—blown up to what seemed to be an uncommon print size.

Halfway through the album, was a picture of a girl—aged about eight—seated on the wrought iron bench at the Western Gazebo. I was intrigued.

'Anupama.' Chaaya cut me off before I even started.

'OK. Lovely picture—but how did she end up in this book?'

'She stayed at the lodge with her family for a week. Her parents spent a fair bit of time separately—mostly drinking gin in the lobby or on the side lawn. She wandered up the mountain and found me taking pictures just as you did the other day. I don't know what the deal was with her parents, but she seemed lonely—as if she badly needed a friend. I let her hang around in the front office where she began to behave as if she were my assistant—directing the wait-staff, bellhops, and housekeepers, handling guests—which, in retrospect, she actually did better than most professionals. She would pester me to take a picture of her.

The day before they were supposed to leave, she comes up to me and says, 'Take my picture—I'm going away tomorrow—you won't see me again. At least with the picture you'll remember me. I took her out to the Gazebo and snapped this.'

She stopped for a sip of her coffee. I couldn't help but notice that she swallowed hard.

'When I got the prints back, I sent one to the address that we had for her family in the hotel's records. Her grandfather called up a month later. The three of them had died in a road accident while driving back to Delhi. He cried over the phone, thanking me for taking that picture and sending it.'

'Oh God, that's terrible.'

'Heartbreaking. It then struck me—maybe there was a time in history when photos told a story—they were unique—a step above fine art—a high-fidelity view of a place or an event preserved for people to experience. However, blame the iPhone, DSLRs, Instagram—whatever—it's not the same anymore. The ease with which photos can be taken, and just the numbers of them out there, have devalued them. They just don't have public value. The only meaning they have is the one that you individually ascribe to them. That photo of Anupama is just the picture of a pretty child to you. To me, it's a sad reminder of a little girl who looked up to me and wanted me to be her best friend. It reminds me that I was foolish to resist giving her a hug, cruel to brush off her attempts to be my friend when she copied my hairstyle and mimicked my posture while walking around the lobby. To her grandfather, it's a message from beyond the grave—a keepsake that will keep him going until he meets her in his model of the afterlife.'

I looked back at the photograph. Anupama had a light blush—of course, she was happy that her friend was finally taking a picture of her. Her slender fingers curled over a moulded detail at the corner of the bench. The evening light shone across her face—delicately illuminating her skin with the flattering contrast of soft shadows. The orange rays of the setting sun shone across her brown eyes adding a peculiar twinkle, but the sadness in them was undeniable.

Her hair was pulled back with a broad white headband that emphasised her features.

'I've never seen you wear your hair like that.'

'I can't anymore. I can't look in the mirror if I do. You see it differently now, don't you?' She picked up a paper serviette from the table and reached forward to dab the corner of my left eye. 'You do. You're an empath.'

'No. It's just...' my voice cracked as a cloud of sadness came over me. 'It's just a really sad thing.'

The next picture was one of Doctor Bhatnagar and a woman I assumed to be his wife. Perhaps again it was the film that Chaaya used—the rich colour tones, their uninhibited smiles, it seemed as if Chaaya had frozen a single frame of unbridled joy in that one picture. A richness seemed to emanate from the big red bindi on Mrs Bhatnagar's forehead and percolate through the entire picture.

'Doctor and Mrs Bhatnagar?'

'Yes.' She smiled.

I realised that after Anupama, the pictures in the album ceased to be of trees and grass—there were more people—children, couples, animals—a particularly warming one of a brown and white puppy sleeping on a sofa in the lobby of Baxter Lodge.

'So, Anupama changed the photos that you value.'

'I guess so. I think all us photographers take photos from a basic need to hold on to something fleeting. I think Anupama triggered that in me. I'm sure that if you look deeper, you'll discover something similar about your reasons for buying a camera.'

We sat there for a while, talking about her pictures, my cameras, and Baxter Lodge. I was working hard on being present. She was gorgeous—sitting there in her green cardigan worn over a white blouse, brown flannel skirt, and white tennis shoes. She exuded an old-world elegance that seemed right at home in Baxter Lodge or indeed this cottage. I wanted a picture.

'Chaaya. I want to take a picture of you right there.'

'Sure, but there are conditions.'

'What conditions?'

'You're going to turn off the LCD on your camera—you'll take just one shot and put your camera away—just like with film.'

'What if the picture doesn't come out well?'

'Then you'll have to take another one the next time that I come over.'

'OK.' I had to agree.

'You are planning to invite me over again, aren't you?'

'Yes, of course!'

I brought out the camera with the Helios lens attached. As she demanded, I turned off the LCD screen. I positioned her to try and get the light across her face—the Rembrandt technique—as we photographers call it. I focused—click—it was done. I put the camera away.

Chaaya picked up her album and got to her feet.

'Back to work for me,' she said. 'I'm taking Thursday off to get some pictures of the lilies on the hillside below

Baxter Lodge. Would you like to join me?'

It didn't even take me a second to decide. 'Yes. of course.'

'Same camera rules as today. Meet me at the Baxter Lodge gate at 4.45 am.'

I walked her to the front gate wondering how the hell I would wake up early enough to be at Baxter Lodge at 4.45 am.

As soon as she was out of sight, I went back into my room and plugged the camera into my MacBook.

The photo was nothing as I remembered her.

Perhaps it was a gust of wind the moment that I released the shutter—a lock of hair curled under her left cheek and emphasised her eyes, and her slightly parted lips gave her that cover girl look. Thanks to the Helios lens, the background was a pink and yellow swirl from the bougainvillea and laburnum. This picture—slightly overexposed, but with ample contrast thanks to Fuji's vivid colours—was now one of my favourite pictures ever.

She was right about one thing though—to anyone else, this would be just the picture of an attractive woman—it would fit right in on a newspaper advertisement for bank loans, eyeliner, or Baxter Lodge.

But to me it represented a woman I desire, a desire that grows each moment that we spend together.

Chapter 3

Baxterpur is pitch dark at 4.15 am.

I had borrowed a large flashlight from Som for the walk to Baxter Lodge. It's interesting how lighting changes everything—the hills that are warm, welcoming, and romantic under the spring sun turn into ominous shadows just within vision. The sky, pitch black, dotted with stars, adds some contrast. But the sense of foreboding remains.

The stars. I've never seen so many stars. I don't know, maybe it was all those years of living in polluted cities like Bangalore and Delhi where you never really see the sky, or maybe just life's general preoccupations that prevented me from connecting with the beauty that was all around me.

I reached the guard house of Baxter Lodge at 4.30 am. I had just about seated myself on a rock beside it when the beam of a flashlight danced around a bend in the road and a briskly walking figure came into view.

It was her.

We started down a goat path beside the guard house. It felt brave—walking down a steep gravelly hill path in pitch darkness with two flashlights. I remembered this slope—daunting even in broad daylight. Chaaya, though, manoeuvred it with a practised ease, knees bent, using her two cameras as a counterweight.

The darkness began to ease.

Twenty minutes later, we arrived at flat rock. Chaaya sat down on the rock and extracted a thermos flask and two tin cups from her backpack. She poured out two cups of milky coffee and handed me one.

'What—no fir trees this time?'

'Haha, cute.'

The sky started to turn purple over the hills. The purple blended into pink, and then a tide of light poured over the ridge, bathing the valley in a rose gold shine. I sat there with Chaaya—taking in the sight—I remembered a Facebook post about life not being about the number of breaths that you take, but about the moments that take your breath away. This was life—the intensity of this arousal that comes entirely from the glands—coupled with the emotion that this awesome show of nature inspired. Impossible to articulate.

Impossible.

'True. It's all about the moments that take your breath away.'

She was so close I could feel her words on my cheek

and smell the coffee on her breath. I could have kissed her.

'Sorry, did I think aloud?'

'No, but I think anyone with a speck of humanity in them would have that thought in this moment. And you're an empath.'

We sat there watching the valley light up.

'Tell me about the lilies.'

'Well, nothing much to say, they're delicate looking flowers that are actually quite tough. They bloom in spring and fill the entire valley with their fragrance. They endure through the summer and wither in the monsoon. The winter freezes their bulbs in the soil—but come spring, up they come again.'

'Why are they important to photograph?'

'Well, they are pretty. In this setting, more so. You'll see.'

We walked deeper into the valley to a patch of white lilies. I knelt at the edge—they were small flowers with slender petals, translucent in the morning sun. The cool mountain air, the light fragrance of the lilies—this was all something new—much better than day-drinking up at Hillcrest cottage.

Chaaya shot pictures of the lilies, while I shot pictures of her. Somewhere along the way, she took a large pink lily and put it in the hair above her left ear. She worked leisurely, taking her time to set up her tripod and camera, looking at the flowers from various angles, occasionally taking a reading with an analogue light meter.

The lilies were gorgeous in their natural setting. The sight of the early morning sun on the delicate petals was ethereal. Were you to sit there and just stare, they drew you in.

I kept my promise to her. I switched off the camera's display and shot pictures of her among the lilies. I didn't get to see what those pictures looked like. I liked the thought of shooting on film even more.

By 10 am, the valley was flooded with bright sun. Chaaya and I returned to the rock. She emptied the contents of her backpack, sorted her films, and reloaded her cameras. She then took out a box of sandwiches and two cans of coke.

'Breakfast,' she announced.

I could use breakfast. The only nourishment I'd had that day was the cup of coffee that Chaaya had poured out for me in the morning. After we finished our sandwiches, she took out a pair of binoculars and scanned the valley.

'Let's continue,' she said and got to her feet.

This time was a little different though. Instead of wandering between the patches of lilies, she marched straight down into the valley—there was a sense of purpose and direction this time. I had a sense of foreboding—something like the anxiety that struck me the other afternoon at Dwidala Camera Shop. She seemed to have sensed it.

'You're going to see something amazing.'

'What?'

'You'll see.'

Walking along the floor of the valley, we came to a rocky crevice that ran steeply up the other side. Chaaya tightened her straps.

The crevice was treacherous—slippery with moss. A damp smell evoked the sense of being in a tropical rainforest. Even the grass and plants were different from those we had seen in the valley all morning. I wondered where we were heading—I was getting hungry for lunch and with the slippery climb, progress was slow.

Slices of experience.

I took in the smells, the sounds, the stick insects, lizards, wild berries, toadstools…the sense of Chaaya's powerful presence had actually begun to fade.

We ascended about a hundred metres—almost vertically—and the crevice opened up into a cavern of sorts. Orchids grew at the rim of this cave—their delicate stringy roots dangling all the way to the mossy floor. Beautiful flowers—long white petals with pale blue specks and a brilliant yellow centre. Chaaya was right. This was something extraordinary.

I looked at her—she was rooted to her spot—mesmerised by something ahead. I followed her gaze.

About six feet inside the cavern, three large luminescent lilies rose on slender stalks from a glistening bed of leaves.

The lilies had floppy gold petals that transitioned to a dark purple towards the calyx. The stalks were a glossy dark green with blood red flecks. The narrow leaves were light green, with yellow streaks. I had never seen anything like this in my life.

'Oh wow.' No other words could describe this sight.

'Yes.' Her voice was barely a whisper.

Chaaya took out her iPhone and took one picture of the lilies.

I raised my camera and was stepping forward for a picture when Chaaya's hand clamped onto my shoulder.

'No, don't go closer. Not Now. Please.'

'OK. Can I take a picture from here?'

'Yes.'

I knelt where I was and took a picture of the lilies framed perfectly centre.

'Let's go,' said Chaaya.

'What?'

'Yes. We'll be back. I promise.'

'Oh, come on. We've walked half a day to get here.' I might have sounded like a wheedling schoolboy, but the exertion of the climb was really getting to me.

'Please.'

'OK.' I raised the camera to my eye to take another picture.

'You've already got one. We'll be back soon.'

'Are you serious? You haven't taken any pictures

on your cameras either.'

'You'll soon see that all of this is worth more than any number of pictures—more than you can ever comprehend.'

Something inside me wanted to call her out for spouting the gibberish that Lama Phuntsok and that camera monk were proficient in. I paused—seeing something in her eyes.

I put down my camera and followed her.

Instead heading back down, we continued up the crevice. About fifty metres further up, Chaaya found a goat path that ran parallel to the valley and cut through a pass to join the Baxterpur road. Two hours later, in fading light, we found ourselves at a tea stall on the Baxterpur road—pretty much in the middle of nowhere.

We sat on dangerously brittle plastic chairs at a sun-bleached plastic table. It had been hours since breakfast—I was famished, weary, and my legs burned from all the climbing and walking. Chaaya looked tired too—she had a light sunburn, but her eyes had an electric energy—as if she was inspired by something in that flower.'

'So, what now?'

'I'll get food and ask Bhishambar to come and pick us up.'

She summoned the stall keeper and asked him for soft drinks and masala Maggi noodles with eggs. The man brought us tepid bottles of Coca Cola that overflowed when he opened them.

While she spoke to Bhishambar, I tried to focus on my slices of experience—the gentle whisper of the mountain breeze; the hiss of the kerosene pump stove; the appetizing smell of the Maggi tastemaker that's familiar to every Indian 80s child—and Chaaya. I looked into her eyes—trying to comprehend that storm that seemed to swirl in them.

'That was the Boadicea lily.' She paused, as if expecting a response.

'I saw the Sentinel orchids from the rock when I was surveying the mountain, and I had to go and check it out. I'm sorry the day was longer than you expected.'

'That's not a problem—it's not that I had anywhere to be. Also, I have no idea why the Boadicea lily and Sentinel orchids are important.'

Her phone chimed. She picked it up, looked at it for a second, and set it down.

'I want you to come back there with me tomorrow. I'll send the jeep to pick you up at 9.'

'Why don't we do an early morning thing like today?'

'Someone else will be joining us.'

The food arrived.

It was a decade since I'd tasted Maggi noodles. The ubiquitous instant noodles had been a staple for me in my engineering college days. It's popular with roadside stall keepers because you only need hot water to prepare it—the addition of eggs or vegetables improves its taste by magnitudes.

Mine was curried with eggs, onions, tomatoes, green chillies, and cilantro. Somewhere between graduating from college; seven years as a low-level tech employee; the years of balancing a full-time job with an entrepreneurial venture; three years as an actual CEO, I had forgotten how good this tasted. Just like all those years ago, I was sliding into that sublime, albeit bloated joy that only Maggi masala noodles could bring.

There's something about Baxterpur. Despite coming here for Lama Phuntsok's workshop that didn't really work for me, so many other things were happening—Chaaya, the monk, and now this Boadicea lily and its Sentinel orchids.

Chaaya gestured to the stall keeper—smoking an invisible cigarette with her left hand.

The stall keeper brought over two battered cigarettes—pre-rolled hashish joints that were sold in tea shops all around Baxterpur. Chaaya lit the joint and took a deep drag. I watched as the orange glow illuminated her eyes. She offered it to me.

'No thanks. I don't smoke dope.'

'Oh, come on Harish, you can't come to Baxterpur for a meditation workshop and not smoke BP.'

'BP? What the hell is that?'

'Baxterpur Peach—that's what this is called on the international market.'

'What? We have an internationally famous type of hashish?'

'From across India there may be at least ten.' She took another drag.

'Why is this called Peach?'

'Find out for yourself,' she said, holding out the joint.

My experience with smoke has mostly been the fruity sheesha when out with my team in Delhi. I used to smoke cigarettes in college, and perhaps smoked marijuana once. But hell.

I took the joint from her and took a drag. Then another—a slower, deliberate one. I felt the fatigue evaporate from my body—replaced with a languid awareness—a pulsing action, activity, aliveness—a lazy aliveness.

I get it.

The smoke was a bit peachy—I mean in a sour sort of way. I mean it was smoke, somewhat fruity, not like a sheesha fruity, no no. Like dry, hot smoke—not like a sheesha's smoke, which is wet and heavy, but like a cigarette's smoke that is sort of dry you know, but sour. Not so much like a peach, but a fruity sour, that actually could be an unripe peach from some perspectives.

Chaaya giggled. 'Lift off! Look at you, Mr Arya! Flying after two hits! Now give it back.'

'Wait—I'm just trying to figure out the peach bit.' I took another drag. 'I mean it's fruity, but...'

'Pass it back—that's cannabis etiquette.'

'OK'. My throat felt dry in any case.

The stall keeper brought me a glass of tea. The sugar from the super-sweet milky tea hit the sourness on my tongue. Peach. Definitely peach. The tea sent another wave of awareness through my body.

The jeep from Baxter Lodge arrived. Chaaya paid the stall keeper and we slid into the rear seats. She dropped the second joint into my shirt pocket. 'You'll enjoy this more than I will,' she whispered.

I felt the ride, and like how.

The jeep, growling along the meandering hill road, swinging around hairpin bends, certainly took every cell of my being along. I mean how often does anything make you feel this way? When you ride in a car, or a boat, or a rollercoaster, you always feel a part of it. But this feeling—deep down inside the feeling of being taken along—each and every piece of you—including your soul is transported through the cool, pine scented air with the mild hint of diesel smoke.

Or maybe it's just that I was stoned as hell and Bhishambar is a crappy driver.

We reached Hillcrest Cottage.

'Tomorrow, 9 am.' Chaaya reminded me.

'What's happening tomorrow at 9 am?'

She snapped her fingers twice before my face 'Bhishambar will come to pick you up. We're going back to the Boadicea lily.'

'Oh, yes, yes of course. OK.'

Chapter 4

The next morning, while I was having breakfast outdoors, a large black and red helicopter flew low over Hillcrest cottage. Bad news for my breakfast—its wash blew the bread and cheese slices off my table. Flying lower, the chopper disappeared around the hill, a rude disturbance to a placid mountain morning.

These fucking Delhi billionaires, I tell you.

I had barely finished my coffee when I heard a horn from the main gate. Bhishambar was there with the Baxter Lodge jeep. Nine o'clock on the dot—just as Chaaya had said.

The short jeep ride through the spring morning was pleasant, and over too soon. Chaaya was waiting for me in the lobby of Baxter Lodge.

'Coffee before we start?'

'Sure.'

She walked to the coffee machine and made two cappuccinos.

I remembered the day when I fainted in this place and felt a tinge of embarrassment.

'I hope I don't faint today.'

She smiled and took a thoughtful sip from her cup. It seemed as if she wanted to say something but then she changed her mind.

'Say it.'

'No. I'd rather you experience it.'

'What. Come on. Now you have me thinking.'

She smiled, holding me in place with her eyes, her face glowing with mischief.

I took my time finishing my coffee—sip by sip—but this time I had Chaaya sitting across from me, her impish eyes gleaming…but why?

'Follow me,' she said, rising to her feet.

I obeyed.

We headed up the grand staircase. As we passed the bay windows on the landing, I caught sight of the black and red helicopter parked on the rear lawn.

Chaaya led me to a room on the second floor and knocked on the door.

An oriental looking man in a black suit opened the door.

'Adachi San,' Chaaya said bowing.

'Chaaya San,' he replied returning the bow.

She pointed to me with a sort of sideways karate chop gesture. 'Harish Arya.'

'Harish San,' he said bowing again, then stepped aside from the door to let us pass.

I was wondering what was going to happen next when I saw him.

Hiroto Soga.

Forty Billion US Dollars sitting casually on a couch in a guest house in Uttarakhand.

'So, this is the friend you have been rambling around the hills with,' he said in Oxford English, with the slightest nip of Japanese intonation.

Chaaya smiled. 'Yes. He was with me when I found the lily.'

'Mr Arya, please, please be seated.'

'Please call me Harish, Mr Soga.' I said while lowering myself onto the couch.

'Then you must call me Hiroto. You shouldn't have sold Linguintel to Akshay Bhalla. You should have sold it to me. But that's something we will discuss later.'

'You know each other?' Chaaya asked.

'Not really,' I said. 'Hiroto's private equity fund was investing heavily in Indian companies. They were interested in the company that I sold to Shaybee Ventures—Akshay Bhalla's firm—we've never met though.'

'Wow. Small world', Chaaya said.

'We have other business,' Hiroto said. 'Are we ready?'

'Yes,' Chaaya replied.

'Bushida, Adachi,' Hiroto called, 'let's go.'

Adachi walked into the room—he had changed into hiking attire with one of those jackets sporting a dozen pockets, cargo pants, and boots. Another Japanese man—similarly attired, who I assumed was Bushida, also entered. Unlike them, Hiroto wasn't dressed for the occasion. He wore khaki trousers, a pale blue linen shirt, and brown boat shoes.

Bushida handed him an alpine stick and we headed out of Baxter Lodge. We made an unusual sight—Chaaya in the lead with her hat and sunglasses, Hiroto following a step behind, Adachi and Bushida just behind him, wearing backpacks and Adachi holding what looked like a large metal suitcase.

About an hour of walking later, we found ourselves at the base of the crevice. It was warming up and the exertion showed. Hiroto had patches of dampness at his armpits and Chaaya's face was covered with a sweaty sheen. Adachi and Bushida had some colour to their cheeks.

'Up there,' Chaaya said.

'Couldn't you have told me that I was wearing the wrong shoes?' Hiroto said to her. It was unclear if he was annoyed or fake annoyed behind his sunglasses.

'Did you bring the right shoes?' Chaaya shot right back—she held power over him—how often do you see the manager of a hotel retort to a mythical technology billionaire?

Hiroto cracked a smile below his sunglasses. 'Let's go.'

We had maintained the marching order that we started at the hotel with. It struck me—are Bushida and Adachi Ninjas or something else?

Ascending the precarious slope, Adachi appeared to be holding a position at Hiroto's left knee. Bushida was level with his right heel. Ever so often, Adachi would touch Hiroto with just two fingers—sometimes the knee, sometimes just at the base of his spine. I realised he was discreetly steadying him as he climbed. One time Bushida held his heel when Hiroto reached high while climbing. These two though, never seemed off balance or exerted. The other details fell in place—the calloused knuckles common on Karatekas; tight facial skin like you see on high-performance athletes; the relative ease with which they were making this climb. Definitely bodyguards of some sort—definitely not the kind of chunky duffers that follow Akshay Bhalla around.

I was worn out in more ways than one. I'm not used to such exertion—all I wanted to do was indulge my crush on Chaaya and there I was—climbing a hill in the middle of nowhere—with a billionaire, two ninjas, and a woman—who now seemed painfully out of reach. There's this funny way how emotion weighs on you. Whether the helicopter on the lawn; Hiroto's reference to the fire-sale of Linguintel to Akshay Bhalla; or the lover-like banter between Chaaya and Hiroto—a cluster of emotions was building up inside me like a heavy rock.

I just wanted to head back to Hillcrest cottage and smoke that Baxterpur Peach that was lying on my dresser.

We reached the lily.

Hiroto stood there, hands on his hips, taking in the sight. Both Adachi and Bushida were down a knee—digging into their backpacks.

Adachi pulled three T-shaped implements out of his bag. They seemed familiar, but I couldn't place them. He put on surgical gloves and plastic shoe covers and took a position behind Hiroto. Bushida too, put on gloves and shoe covers, and pulled out a gleaming steel trowel.

The lilies were just as beautiful as I remembered them—ethereal petals on stalks of light, floating in this dark cave.

Hiroto dropped his hands.

'Hajime.'

Adachi reverently stooped towards the lilies, and extended a metal measuring tape towards the stalks. Measuring about three feet from the base, he rammed one of the steel Ts into the ground. I then realised what they were—soil sampling tubes that I had seen on a TV programme years ago. He stuck another one in about the two-feet mark, and the third closer—near the base of the stalks—gently moving the leaves to avoid bruising them.

He retrieved the tubes, wrote on the handles with a marker pen, and put them in individual plastic bags.

Bushida then advanced on his hands and knees, gently

loosening the soil with his trowel. I watched as he worked in a slow circle around the plants. In a few minutes he had loosened all three stalks.

The metal suitcase was some sort of refrigerated carrier. He cut the flowers off the stalks with what seemed to be a super-sharp tanto-style knife and placed each in a glass jar. He then rummaged through the mass of soil and roots at the end of the stalks and was able extract about eight bulbs from them. These too, he deposited in a single glass jar. He stacked all the jars in the suitcase, and wiped the mud off each side of the trowel with a swipe of his index finger, and cleaned his hands and the tool with several white towels that he then stowed away in a plastic bag, which he placed in his backpack.

Hiroto put his sunglasses in his shirt pocket and muttered something with his hand outstretched. Bushida handed him the knife—delicately placing the handle in his palm. This whole thing—right from the time Adachi began to measure out the distance from the flowers was like an act in an elaborate ballet—each step planned, rehearsed to perfection, set to a silent beat, with these elegant men keeping time and communicating psychically.

Hiroto looked at the Sentinel orchids growing around the rim of the cave. He put his palm under one of them and cut it off by gently pressing its stalk against the edge of the knife. Bushida took the knife from him.

Hiroto took in the orchid for a few seconds and turned

to Chaaya. He gently put it though a hairclip that she wore above her left ear—she swayed ever so slightly—blushing.

Hiroto put his hands on her shoulders and smiled at her.

'Arigato gozaimasu.'

Adachi and Bushida bowed and repeated the phrase.

We trekked back to the food stall by the Baxterpur road. Bhishambar was waiting there with a silver SUV. Bushida and Adachi put their bags in the back of the vehicle.

We sat in a circle around one of the rickety tables and the stall keeper walked up.

'Masala Ramen everyone?' Chaaya asked aloud.

Hiroto looked at Adachi and Bushida.

'Yes,' we all echoed.

The stall keeper nodded and returned to his stove.

Hiroto smiled at me. 'You're still wondering what's going on.'

'Yes.'

'Well, I collect lilies. What we saw there—the Boadicea lily—is a rare flower. It's just so hard to find one—that too in full bloom. Myrtle Edith Bromley—an amateur botanist—who lived here in the late 1800s first documented them. She made a series of eleven drawings of the lilies as they bloomed and wilted. The pictures—highly detailed watercolours that included the Sentinel orchids, were then dismissed by the East Indian Lilium Society as the fatuous doodling of a bored housewife.'

'Fucking typical,' Chaaya muttered.

In the 1930s a British military officer encountered it and was told of its use in local mystical practices. It's been sighted perhaps four times since Mrs Bromley sketched it. Attempts were made twice to collect it, which unfortunately failed—I'm hoping that I succeed.'

'That's an interesting story,' I said. 'Is this lily always seen with the Sentinel orchid?'

Hiroto nodded. 'Yes, in all recorded instances since the Bromley sketches.'

'Then why didn't you collect the orchids too? Perhaps there's a—what do they call it—symbiotic relationship there. I vaguely recall something like that from high-school biology—where two species have a critical dependency on each other.'

Hiroto froze. His eyes dropped to focus on a spot on the table. He pursed his lips and turned to look at Adachi.

Adachi rose to his feet. 'Bushida. Ik'zo.'

The two of them walked to the Land Cruiser, retrieved the backpacks and the suitcase, and headed back up the mountain.

'Thank you,' Hiroto said, looking at me.

The stall keeper brought us the masala ramen, and masala ramen would be the appropriate term. Soupy Maggi noodles in a bowl with two soft boiled eggs on the top, garnished with finely chopped green chillies, caramelised onion, ginger, garlic, and cilantro.

He told Chaaya that he would bring food for the other two '*sahibs*' when they returned.

I looked at the gaunt stall keeper in his faded clothes, with his weatherbeaten face and rough hands. A part of me wondered how those gnarled hands could put together something as elegant as this. This trip to Baxterpur was rapidly escalating into a series of surprises.

The stall keeper waited, looking expectantly at Hiroto.

'*Itadakimasu,*' Hiroto said to him with folded hands.

He then picked up chopsticks and prodded one of the eggs—it split and a creamy yolk oozed out. He lifted a clump of noodles through the yolk and stuck them in his mouth. He took a good twenty seconds to finally swallow.

He flashed the stall keeper a broad smile. 'Good, very good! Thank you!'

Hiroto turned to me. 'The biggest problem in this world is the epidemic of low expectations. People always rise—or fall to what you expect from them.'

'You've been here before?'

'Many times.' He smiled at me.

The stall keeper had served my Ramen with a fork and spoon. I asked him for chopsticks.

'Are you sure Bushida and Adachi will be OK up there? I mean it will be dark soon and these mountains are hazardous even in broad daylight.'

Hiroto smiled at me. 'They know what they're doing.'

'So, what's the big deal with this lily? Why would you

fly in on a helicopter and trek all the way up this mountain to collect three flowers?'

'A link to my past, perhaps. My family has always collected lilies. During the Second World War, much of that collection—going back generations—was lost. My great-grandmother rebuilt much of that collection during the last few years of her life. She died in her greenhouse among the lilies in full bloom. During my early years, I would sit with her, listen to stories of her days before the war and read through the books about flowers—many that were over a hundred years old.'

We ate and sat there, mostly in silence, until Adachi and Bushida returned about four hours later. The stall keeper brought us another round of masala ramen and coke, which we ate by the light of an electric lantern that he placed in the centre of our table.

'Time to memorialise this adventure,' Hiroto announced once we were done eating.

Adachi left the table and returned with a camera and a tripod.

A film camera and a tripod.

Chapter 5

I woke up to a message from Chaaya asking if I was free for dinner with Hiroto.

My body was still aching from the previous day's trek, and I was hoping to smoke some of that Baxterpur Peach and just relax on the rear lawn.

But still I replied I was free, and she messaged back saying she would send the jeep for me at six. Six seemed a bit early for dinner, but I didn't protest.

I walked into the lobby of Baxter Lodge at about 6.15 pm. Chaaya met me and led me back up to the room where we had met Hiroto the previous morning. Hiroto, Bushida, and Adachi were there, sitting around the coffee table.

A camp stove was on the coffee table, with a bubbling pot of yak butter tea. I had grown used to the smell over the past few weeks, and had even begun to enjoy it. This was unusual though—I had expected dinner with a

Japanese billionaire would involve a round of overrated Japanese whisky or nearly-as-overrated Japanese gin—but yak butter tea?

Bushida was sitting at one corner of the table grinding the contents of a blue and white porcelain bowl with a wooden pestle.

'Japanese tea ceremony?' I joked.

Hiroto tossed his head back with a chuckle. 'No, no, no. It's a Baxterpur tea ceremony.'

I looked to Chaaya. 'What's that?'

She smiled at me. 'We're making tea, and then we'll drink it.'

'What about dinner?'

'We'll have dinner afterwards.'

Satisfied with the contents of the bowl, Bushida tipped it into the simmering yak butter tea. Hiroto reached under the table—brought out a chopping board, a santoku knife, and a glass jar with a Boadicea lily in it.

He placed the lily on the cutting board and cut it into tiny strips—in slow, measured strokes, and added the pieces to the simmering broth. Adachi stirred the pot with a wooden ladle and then turned off the flame.

I had been silent for most of this show. I looked at Chaaya.

She smiled at me. 'You'll have to see for yourself. No explanation will be enough.'

I looked at Adachi. He just smiled at me and nodded ever so slightly.

Chaaya sat beside me on the couch. 'You're safe here.'

'So, what is this?' I asked, 'this whole thing is absurd—I'm still trying to make sense of what's been happening the past few days.'

'Well, life is full of occurrences,' said Hiroto. 'You stayed at Baxter Lodge, Chaaya likes you, so she asked you to join her while she photographed the lilies. The two of you found the Boadicea lily, and now I'm here. And now we're all here. You, me, Chaaya, Bushida, Adachi—we're all here, in this moment, because of a random chain of events. It's a mesh of tiny coincidences involving time, hearts, glands, a Land Cruiser, and a helicopter. You're here. Now. That's all that matters.'

'Okay,' I said. I wasn't sure I even knew what I meant.

That seemed to be Bushida's cue. He walked into the next room and rolled in a wooden trolley loaded with white towels and porcelain.

He set five places at the coffee table—neatly folded towels with a delicate porcelain cup placed upside down at its centre. He rolled a damp towel, coiled it into a circular pad, and placed it at the centre of the table. Grabbing the pot, he placed it on the rolled towel and moved the stove to the trolley.

Hiroto stirred the pot gently and seemed pleased with the texture of its contents. Walking around the table, he filled all the bowls to the brim and returned to his place at the head of the table—filling his own cup last. They watched their cups silently for about a minute, perhaps waiting for the contents to cool or maybe engaged in a deeper contemplation of what the cup held for them.

'I'll go first,' Chaaya said. She lifted her cup and took a sip. She smiled, licked her upper lip, took a second, longer sip. A blush came to her cheeks. She drained her cup and then sat back.

'Come on Harish.'

I lifted my cup. The tea was hot, but not uncomfortably so. I took a sip. Creamy and fragrant—like the yak butter tea that you get all over Baxterpur—but tasted strongly of Baxterpur Peach. Like Chaaya, I drained my cup in three sips and then sat back. I felt the familiar warmth of the butter tea sitting in my chest.

Wait a minute—did Hiroto say that Chaaya likes me?

The warmth from the tea began to spread through my body. I could feel my breath expand—like it was filling my torso, legs, arms, face…my whole body felt as if it was expanding and contracting with my breath. This felt weird. It felt scary.

'Relax. Don't fight it,' came Chaaya's voice.

Hands I didn't see laid me flat on the couch with my head in Chaaya's lap. They placed my hands together over my stomach, and she rested her hand over mine. The dry warmth of her palm was comforting. I looked up at her. She was leaning back on the couch, still, her eyes closed. I could see the vein in her neck pulsing.

My mind began to blur. The sense of my entire body expanding and contracting with my breath was overwhelming. With each inhale, I swelled up like a balloon; with each exhale I shrank. But there was Chaaya—eyes closed, a faint smile, a light blush on her cheeks.

I closed my eyes and surrendered to the sensation. For a few moments I wanted to control it—holding my breath to control the bloating—as if it was some physical fatness that I was ashamed of. I couldn't hold my breath. With the next gusty inhale, I blew up to the size of the couch we were on. Exhale—I shrank back to my size. This I could handle. With the next inhale, I felt my body growing again. I held my breath—tight.

Perhaps a minute passed and I had to breathe. Inhale again—I grew to the size of the Land Cruiser. Exhale—I shrank to the size of the blue cushion on the couch. Another inhale, and I blew up to the size of the helicopter on the green lawn. Exhale—I shrunk to the size of the pot of Boadicea tea. Inhale—I blew up to the size of Baxter Lodge—floating like a blimp in a golden darkness or a dark goldness. You'll never picture it right anyway. Exhale—I shrunk to the size of the quarter carat diamond in Chaaya's nose pin.

I felt her hand on mine and her soft voice— 'I'm here. We're here. Don't fight it. Give in.'

I let go.

On the next inhale, I grew bigger than the couch,

the Land Cruiser, the helicopter, Baxter Lodge, the Taj Mahal—bigger than anything man has ever made. I was in the golden blackness, floating like a planet blimp.

And then light—oh the light—the beach. My Daadiji, my darling Daadiji on the beach in Bombay. My mother forbade her from taking me out in the summer sun, but we had driven down to Chowpatty in her rickety Standard Gazelle and sat in the boiling heat. She told me about her lovely house in Peshawar—the beige building with turrets, battlements, latticework balconies—and the high door step so that horsemen could step off their stirrups and into the house. The lavish cruises she had taken on the Queen Mary, City of Paris, and Orion, and that last cruise in 1947—from Karachi to Bombay—when she was allowed just one suitcase. I was seven years old and I didn't know then why talking of that last cruise made her cry.

'Bend over and take it like a man, Arya.' The business end of the hockey stick bit into my buttocks.

'Again,' came Parag Zain's voice. The hockey stick hit again, and I cried.

'What a fucking pansy you are.' Zain's voice mocked me. 'I'm disappointed. I always thought you were a proper guy. Bend.'

This time he kicked me with his parade boots. A hundred such assaults—belts, soccer shoes, curtain rods, wet towels—everything that the Head Boy and Prefects of the Craddyck Boys' School were allowed to administer in the name of discipline.

'Stay with the Good,' came Chaaya's voice.

The Golden Blackness enveloped me again. My body still pulsed with my breath. What was this blackness? A sense of warmth and a gentle darkness, that a light from far away seemed to permeate. A celestial womb?

I felt an icy gust of wind and my feet felt cold. I was on a mountain ridge marching in line to Manirang peak. The thin air and biting cold were ravaging my 13-year-old body.

'Man up, Arya!' bellowed the expedition leader. 'If you drop out of this one, the entire team goes back and nobody gets to Manirang pass.

One of the porters intervened, asking the rest of the party to proceed.

He sat me down on a rock and put his arm around me as I caught my breath. He smelt of stale tobacco and goats but there was a reassuring warmth about his embrace. He reached into his coat and extracted what looked like a two-inch long twig. He drew his *khukree* and peeled it. When done, he stuck it into my mouth and asked me to chew.

'*Pahari davai hai yeh. Chabao aur ras piyo*.'

I obeyed him. I chewed the twig and swallowed the juice. I felt the numbness and fatigue in my body ease. The world came into focus and I felt as if I'd just taken off fogged glasses. My heart rate slowed and my body filled with an electric energy. The tobacco and goat smell from the porter became overpowering and I recoiled involuntarily. He cackled, exposing a row of tobacco-stained teeth and patted my back.

'Chalo.'

We caught up with the group in a few minutes. I wasn't tired anymore. The twig was bitter—the kind of bitterness that transitions to a bitter sweetness—you know—like beer.

We're celebrating Linguintel's first round of funding—4S, Defence Colony—ice cold Kingfisher beer, spicy tandoori food, music too loud to talk over. Ten million Indian rupees—an unimaginable sum of money in the early years of India's startup boom. I finally have a salary—One lakh rupees a month. Too little for a CEO, I later discover—but well.

We drink, and we drink—and we drink. My girlfriend Sameera gets me home somehow.

I blew up again in the golden blackness. Bunky the Purple Monkey floated nose to nose with me. He was as big as me, purple, with a brown face, impish eyes, a wide smile and a little pink tongue sticking out at the left corner of his mouth. His black bead eyes were far apart because his face is 10 times wider than mine. He spoke with the voice of a child.

'You did nothing.'

'What could I have done?'

'Something.'

'There was nothing I could do.'

'She took Srishti away and you did nothing.'

The huge nothingness felt like an immense hollowness. A hollowness rapidly filling with a burning lava of shame.

'There was nothing I could do!' I howl.

Bunky the Purple Monkey expanded. His eyes grew to the size of jet engines—his face was as wide as a football field. The fur on his head was matty like lawn grass. He floated lower. The monk somersaulted on his head—looking at me eye-to-eye.

'The shame is nothing,' he said.

'What?'

'Let it go. Whether there was something you could do, or something that you couldn't—it doesn't matter anymore. The *hollowness* is what you are. The hollowness is what everything is. The nothingness is what we all are. We drink from samsara—fill ourselves with guilt, shame, purpose, love, hate. It's nothing. All an *illusion*.'

'What was that then about taking pictures on film? Freezing a slice of experience?'

'A slice of experience in your world, in your private universe. Right now, I want you to focus. Embrace your nothingness. Let go of the shame.'

The name you give your child has an aspirational element—even a metaphorical import. Srishti—creation—not in the physical or scientific sense, but metaphysically—everything that was, that is, and that ever will be. Everything that could have been, should have been—all in a brown eyed child with shiny black curls. Well, at least that's what she meant to me.

The day I saw that eight-week foetus on a foggy print in a basement clinic in Gurgaon—everything changed. I started running Linguintel like a real business and haggled the valuations with the Private Equity sharkstards who had been circling for months. You'd be surprised how much things change when you get off the phone telling them that you'll 'think about it' and respond two days later with an email thanking them for their time but that you've been offered a term sheet at a 'substantially higher valuation'.

Two years later, she was taken from me. Six weeks later—I sold Linguintel.

I shut my eyes tight, and boiling hot tears rolled down my face. I felt soft hands on my cheeks, the light notes of Guerlain Shalimar, and heard Chaaya's voice.

'It will all be okay,' she said. I saw her eyes through the tears.

The emptiness. Sitting in my apartment in the darkness, speaking to my lawyer about staying out of prison and fighting the cases that Sameera filed against me.

The emptiness—the world began to spin and I started to puke. Strong but gentle hands turned me over, and I retched into a white enamel pan. A warm, moist towel pressed against my chin as my body heaved—as if forever. I felt as if I was expelling an invisible tar.

It stopped. My vision cleared.

Adachi mopped my face with a moist towel. When done, he added it to a pile of puke-covered towels. He bundled them up in a hotel robe and took them away.

The world came back into focus. I was drenched in sweat—hair plastered to my forehead, shirt wet right through. Khakis too.

'I think you need a shower,' Bushida said. He pointed to a door—one of the bedrooms in the suite.

I showered with an electric lightness flowing through my body. A sense of clarity—like wearing new glasses—actually, more like removing a set of glasses and discovering that your eyesight had been great all along and that your glasses had just been blinding you. When I stepped out of the shower, I found a white XL Lacoste T-shirt and a pair of 36-inch waist Marks & Spencer jeans on the bed. Just right for me.

When I stepped back into the hall, Hiroto, Adachi, Bushida, and Chaaya were sitting on stools around the kitchen table.

A large metal pot was on the fire, with the hiss of boiling oil coming from it. Adachi was beating the contents of a white porcelain bowl with chopsticks. I looked at it for a second—I'd had enough of these kooks and their fucking porcelain bowls for seven lifetimes. I sat on the stool beside Chaaya and was overcome by a silent shame—the shame of the guy who threw up and passed out at a party. That had never been me. Except for that one time in college.

'Just in time for some Tempura,' said Hiroto casually, as if nothing had happened.

'OK. I'm doing fine. Thanks for asking.'

'Nobody asked,' Chaaya said, 'and nobody will ask. We'll only speak of it if you do.'

I watched as Adachi tossed a few indeterminate crustaceans into the bowl and stirred its contents.

'Sake?' Bushida asked.

'Sake as in real sake, or a Baxterpur sake that will take me on another crazy trip?'

'Real sake,' Hiroto said. 'Sudo Honke—the best. Well, enough of it and you could be off on another crazy trip, but that would be a terrible waste of really good sake.' I noticed how his English accent was interrupted by Japanese intonation on vernacular words and reappeared effortlessly.

Adachi began to drop the battered crustaceans into the oil. I counted eight hisses.

'Yes, I'll have some sake,' I said.

Bushida placed a lacquered cup on a saucer before me and poured sake until it overflowed.

'So, what just happened?' I asked.

'You drank some Boadicea yak butter tea,' Hiroto said.

'Yes, but this was as if I was being poisoned. All the sickness, the throwing up…did you see that mess? Adachi, I'm sorry. I made a mess that you had to clean up.'

Adachi nodded. 'Someone did it for me. I did it for

you. One day you'll do it for someone else.'

He took a sizzling tempura from the oil and dropped it on to a saucer before me. I took a sip of the sake. It was delicious. I lifted the shrimp tempura with chopsticks, dipped it in the sauce, and bit into it. Exquisite.

Adachi put the remaining shrimp fritters into a steel colander in the middle of the table and turned to Hiroto. 'Your turn.'

That's how we spent that night. Frying tempura in turns (Bushida and Hiroto taught me how) and drinking sake.

Chapter 6

Back home in the morning, I was stuck in a funk. The lack of sleep and the events of the night made me wonder if I was in some sort of a dream—what was happening to me?

Why did I feel so disconnected from everything? For so many years now, it felt as if this world was unfolding before me like a silent movie—few things got all the way through. Anxiety—when the police came to take me away. Stress—when Akshay Bhalla was playing hard ball on Linguintel's valuation. Emptiness—in my Gurgaon flat, as I strained for the sound of Srishti's laughter. I stayed in there for months, hoping to hear it—just one giggle hiding in a corner somewhere—at the back of a closet, in a bathroom cabinet. But there was just Bunky—sleeping like he used to under the lace-edged napkin that Srishti had taken from her grandmother's dinner set. Just me and Bunky, the Purple Monkey, in there—waiting.

And now there's Chaaya. What did I feel for her?

Honestly? Lust. Just plain visceral lust. The desire to possess something beautiful. Was I really interested in cameras? No. I'm just a technology nerd with three million dollars to throw around. And now there's this monk talking to me about the richness of experience packed into one second. I am thirty-eight-years old—how many seconds of experience have I neglected?

I felt a tightness in my chest—a listlessness, a pointlessness. This wasn't the first time—this sense of desolation has followed me since my childhood. I'd done many things to fill it—and been good at those things: I learned languages, read over a thousand books, started a company and sold it—but at the end of it, I always return to this emptiness. There was something else this time, though—the monk. What did he say—*the hollowness is who I am*? Just what the hell was he doing in my dream?

I picked up my camera bag and took a walk down to the camera shop.

Just like the last time, he was working on a camera under the lamp and magnifying glass in the corner.

'Hello again!' he said, looking up from his work.

'Hello.'

I took in the cameras in the display cabinet. I remember thinking of them as dusty and old, but they weren't. They were shiny and pristine—Canon, Nikon, Yashica, Konica, Leica, Voightlander, Kodak, Agfa…they were names I knew—that I had heard.

'I'm just looking around.'

'That's okay. Feel free to take a closer look at whatever you find interesting.'

'Are you sure? What if something breaks?'

'I'll fix it.'

Yup…Dwidala Camera Shop. The most unusual camera shop on the planet.

This was pointless. I could not use my Fuji lenses on any of these cameras, and I didn't have the slightest clue how to shoot film.

'How do I go about shooting film?'

'Why would you want to shoot film?'

'I don't know.'

'Well, it will all be a waste if there's no intention.'

'I could buy a couple of cameras and just try—perhaps something will inspire me. It won't all be a waste.'

'Ah, the age-old mistake,' the monk said as he walked towards me. His face came into the light. 'Boredom and a lack of intention. Has your Fuji gear inspired you? You have had it for a while and you have made some amazing pictures with it.'

'No, I haven't.'

'Then what makes you think that shooting film will be different?'

'It's back to fundamentals I guess.'

'No, it's not. It's just another box of material possessions that your mortal body will have to carry around—another anchor for your desire that will cause you anxiety—another source of sorrow, envy, inadequacy that will interfere with your experience of *what is*.'

Okay. So that's another way to say you've been offered another term sheet with a substantially higher valuation.

Just then Chaaya entered the shop.

'Oh, Lama Dechen! I see you already have company.'

'Ah!' he exclaimed. 'You divine agent of the universe—as always, your arrival is well timed.'

She made a show of looking at her watch. 'Lunch time?'

Bhikshu Dechen laughed.

'Good one,' he said, still laughing. 'I was asking him why he would want to shoot film.'

'He does?' Chaaya turned to me. 'Harish, why would you want to shoot film?'

'Why do *you* shoot film?' I shot back.

'I think we spoke about this the other day. The suspense of processing and the joy of making something physical?'

She reached into her bag and put five film rolls onto the counter. 'Could you send these down to Dwarkanath?'

'Sure.' The monk took the rolls from her and placed them into one of the compartments in the red cupboard. 'Your fresh film is here.' He opened another compartment and placed a packet of film rolls on the counter.

'So, how would I go about shooting film?'

'You gave him a Helios 44,' Chaaya said to the monk. 'That puts him down the slippery slope of sloppy Soviet cameras. You should have given him a Takumar or Nikkor.'

'Lunch time'. The monk walked to the golden shutter and knocked on it.

Today, there were three stools at the table. As we sat down, the server walked into the shop with three trays of food stacked on his shoulder. Just like the last time—maybe twenty seconds since the monk had knocked on the shutter. Not even enough time to plate the food—load nine bowls, three plates of Shabtra onto trays—then pile it on to one's shoulder.

Pepsi for Chaaya, Canada Dry for me, and water for the monk—and a single Kismi toffee bar.

Right. Another blast from the 1990s. That cloying cardamom-flavoured caramel toffee I used to buy from my school's concessionaire.

'So why do you want to shoot film?' Chaaya asked me.

'I don't know. I'm just curious. I spent a few days with the Helios 44 and I think I really like it. I like the way that it's a bit softer than the Fuji glass—the little imperfections, the way it blurs the background and makes a subject pop.' I pulled out my phone and showed her the picture that I took of her.

'Ooh, this has come out well,' she said and passed the phone to the monk. He looked at it for about ten seconds and nodded.

'What kind of pictures do you like to take?' the monk asked.

'I don't know. Pretty much anything. As you can see, I have the entire Fujifilm lens lineup—I guess I'm ready for everything.'

'What exactly does photography mean to you?' Chaaya asked.

I didn't have an answer to that question. We ate in silence for a few minutes.

'I don't really have an answer to that question,' I said finally.

'I don't know—maybe I wanted to capture a sense of permanence. Lama Dechen, you told me about slices of experience—perhaps that's it. When you've been dealing with the anguish of loss, there's a desire to hold, to preserve. But then there's the digital paradox that you told me about the last time—how many moments can one hoard?'

'I'm a *Bhikshu*, not a *Lama*,' the monk said.

'Do you think he's ready for a film camera?' Chaaya asked the monk.

'He was always ready. He just didn't ask.'

I felt a rage building inside me. What the fuck had this entire conversation been about? I had clearly asked him about shooting film. That's how this conversation started.

The monk was smiling at me. There was a warmth—a kindness—in his eyes that defused my anger. He was right. I asked about shooting film. I did not *'ask'* him for a camera.

'Photography for me, is a struggle for permanence. A desire to capture a slice of experience. I would like a film camera, please.'

Both Chaaya and the monk burst out laughing.

'Oh, come on.' Chaaya slapped my shoulder. 'You're taking this so seriously! God! You're acting like one of Lama Phuntsok's bimbos.'

'Seekers,' the monk corrected her.

'Seriously?' Chaaya asked with an incredulous glare.

'I've been there, Lama Dechen. I've seen them,' I said.

The monk bit into his food chewing it thoughtfully. He swallowed and took a sip of water.

'Ridicule is easy when you view people through the colours of your own illusions—illusions of your own grandeur, importance, and significance. We're all seekers in some way. Some of us don't even know what we are seeking. Even if we try to explain it to others, they wouldn't understand, and if they did, they wouldn't understand what we actually mean.

'Speak to the labourer at the Baxterpur bus stand who unloads luggage for fifteen rupees and tell him about your struggle for permanence. Speak to the boy who cooks your breakfast and tell him about your desire to capture a slice of experience. What do you think they will understand? Given their reality, you will be frivolous—a joke—a caricature of unjust power and advantage.'

He turned to me.

'And you—forget understanding—you don't even listen—she called me Lama Dechen because it is a private joke in our friendship. I corrected you. But you don't see that it's not your place to call me that.'

'I'm sorry.'

'And Phuntsok—he *is* a Lama—a teacher. A man who has devoted fifty years to reflecting and understanding. If you can hold a half-minute conversation with him and understand what he's saying, you will be one of the most aware people in the world. Forget Phuntsok—if you can hold a conversation with anyone, and for just one minute understand exactly what they are saying—what they are truly saying—it's a gift of perception that very, very few people have.'

Chaaya and I stared at our plates in silence.

'Please don't let me ruin your appetite,' he said, after a pause.

Chaaya teased her food with chopsticks. 'I didn't mean like bimbos bimbos, when I referred to them as bimbos,' she mumbled.

'Exactly my point,' the monk said, through a mouthful of food.

Just like the last time, the food was delicious.

'What are your plans for the afternoon?' I asked Chaaya.

'Nothing specific. I may just walk around. What about you?'

'Nothing specific either. Do you want to hang out at Hillcrest?' I suggested.

'That would be a good idea,' the monk said. 'You

could teach him to use the Nikomat.'

'What's a Nikomat?' I asked him.

'You're giving him a Nikomat?' Chaaya asked.

'You suggested that I give him a Nikkor. I think I have a decent 50mm in one of those boxes. Are you envious? If you've had enough of that Canon of yours, I could find one for you too and save you the suffering of covetousness.'

'Tell me about this Nikomat,' I asked him.

'Ooh! FT? FTN? EL? Which one are you giving him?' Chaaya was literally bouncing on her stool.

'FTN.'

'Ooh, so this one, it's a solid metal camera—a tank. Fully mechanical with no electronics at all. When you work the lever to advance the film, it cocks the shutter, arms the mirror— everything. It was made in Japan in the 1960s and I'm sure it still works beautifully. Fantastically engineered.'

'They never cease to amaze me,' the monk said. 'I took this one apart—the shutter speed was still perfectly accurate.'

'A great camera to learn on though,' Chaaya said. 'Because it's completely manual, you'll have to master the art of manual exposure.'

We finished our meal and moved to the counter.

The monk pulled out the Nikomat and a 50mm lens from the red boxes behind him. Looking at them, one wouldn't believe that they were made in the 1960s. Chaaya examined them.

'Where do you get such cool stuff?' she asked.

'The universe has everything you need.'

'He'll also need film.'

'Of course.' He turned to me. 'Would you prefer to shoot colour, or black and white?'

'I've always shot colour, I said, but I've been intrigued by black and white.'

'You'll have to make a decision. Once you have a roll of film in your camera, you can't change anything until you have completed your 36 exposures.'

'Black and white,' I said softly. 'The best way to start I guess.'

'Great decision,' Chaaya said, 'In any case, black and white film is more forgiving of mistakes in exposure.'

She turned to the monk. 'Eastman 5222—five rolls.'

'Five? That's too much.'

'He's a digital shooter. A hundred and eighty frames aren't much.'

The monk opened one of the red boxes, in it was a ziploc with exactly five rolls of film.

'So, what's all of this going to cost me?'

'Do you have anything that you want to let go?' the monk asked.

'Nothing really…perhaps the Fuji 56mm lens that I dropped in the sand a few months ago.'

'Let me see it.'

I rummaged in my bag and found it. My hopes weren't high.

The monk looked at it. 'Pushkar. The sand gets everywhere.'

'Yes, I dropped this one off a camel's back and dug it out of six inches of sand.'

'Ouch,' Chaaya said.

The monk turned the focus ring, and there was the unmistakable sound of sand grinding in the works.

Both Chaaya and I winced.

He looked at the optics. 'Clean lenses. It needs some work, but I think it is salvageable. It seems like a fair trade.'

'Are you serious?' I wondered aloud.

'Yes.'

I looked at Chaaya. She shrugged. I put the camera and lens into my bag and we left the shop after thanking the monk for the meal.

Chaaya and I walked back to Hillcrest. We settled on the couch on the back veranda; she pulled out a joint from her clutch and lit up.

'Weren't you going to teach me how to use my new camera?' I asked her.

'Well, film photography is all about anticipation. Start now—anticipating the joy of using your new Nikomat camera.' She passed me the joint.

'It's hardly new. Made in the 1960s did you say? I'm actually wondering if that was a fair trade.'

'It was more than fair. Did you google your Helios lens?'

'I did.'

We finished the joint and she took out the Kismi toffee bar.

She looked at me mischievously—blushing ever so little—and put her hand on my neck when I leaned in to kiss her.

'This may be the wrong time to clarify this—considering that I've just fucked you out of the friendzone, but why do you sleep with a stuffed monkey?'

'That's Bunky. He belongs to my daughter. That was the only thing left behind when my wife left me, taking her along.'

'Hello Bunky,' Chaaya greeted the monkey by tickling his chin.

I was still tripping from the Baxterpur Peach and the sensations of her body close to mine. The thought of the divorce didn't really descend on me with darkness the way it usually did.

'So, guess you didn't get around to teaching me to use the Nikomat.'

'Not much to learn.'

She rolled out of bed and picked my camera bag. She took out the Nikomat and the packet of film. She examined the lens and pursed her lips.

'Looks brand new—wonder where he gets these from. Maybe I should turn in my Canon one of these days—if he can find me the 55mm Macro lens.'

Loading the film was pretty standard—the way my

mother's Kodak Croma was loaded back in the 1990s. The camera's split screen focusing seemed as if it would take a while to get used to. Chaaya also explained the way the exposure metering worked—balancing a needle between two brackets by adjusting the aperture or shutter speed.

These were the surreal slices of experience. Chaaya explaining this camera to me. I wondered how I got here—in bed, with this beautiful woman—her touch and scent still lingering on my body and my sheets—now punctuated with the pungent oil and old leather smell emanating from this Japanese camera.

'Hello'. She snapped her fingers before my face. 'Are you paying attention?'

'No, sorry, I drifted off for a bit. It's been quite a day.'

'Okay, so if you remember the bit about metering, try taking some pictures. You'll have to keep some notes about shutter speed etc, which will help you when you're looking through these photos later.'

'What about developing?'

'Oh, don't worry—I have all that figured out. Let me know when you're done with the roll.'

She got out of bed and started to get dressed.

'When will I see you again?' I asked her.

'Whenever you like,' she said. 'Do you want to have dinner at my place?'

'Sure.'

It will be really late because I get home only after

ending the dinner service at Baxter Lodge.'

'Suits me. Not like I have to go to the office in the morning.'

After she left, I got busy on my computer. The Nikomat is an old camera, but also terribly common. Nikon made millions of these between 1965 and 1978. The internet forums were full of praise for them—citing resilience, accuracy of the exposure metering system, and the high quality of the 'standard' 50mm f2 lens. Also, my 'Nikomat' was a type that was only available in Japan—the camera was branded 'Nikkormat' for sale overseas. Obviously, the monk had some kind of special supply chain thing going on.

Eastman 5222. This was interesting. This is a film that was designed for motion pictures. According to the internet, movies such as Raging Bull, Schindler's List, and Psycho were shot on it. For decades, high volume shooters such as newspaper photographers have been buying this film in 1000-foot rolls and cutting them down to 36 shot rolls for use in their film cameras. According to people on the internet, the film's fine grain and versatility gives great results.

Dinner was a bit awkward.

Chaaya lived with the doctor and Mrs Bhatnagar as a paying guest. She had obviously been living there for a while as there was a high level of familiarity between them. I was interrogated about my background, professional achievements, personal life—not very discreetly. This was the typical Indian Parent routine—they obviously thought of her as a daughter. Overall, they were a fun, happy couple—exuding the warmth that I had sensed from that picture in Chaaya's album.

It was nearly 4 am when I started off for home. Walking along those mountain roads lit just by a half-moon, I felt a pang of loneliness. I wanted her here, walking beside me—her warm hand in mine, talking to me about the night, the moon, the Nikomat, anything. I wanted to walk home with her and hold her close—surround myself with everything that was good about her—her beauty, kindness, humour. But I had been here before. Ten years ago, I had felt the same for Sameera. It went very well for us. We loved each other, we married, had a child together. Yet one day, she just upped and left—not just my house and my city, but the continent and country. She made doubly sure that I wouldn't be able to follow her.

I felt empty. Drained. It was funny. Here I am, living in a mountain paradise, with enough money in the bank to not work another day for three lifetimes. But yet, this emptiness. I don't remember ever feeling it so deeply. At the outset, this day was amazing. A walk in the sun, banter with the monk and Chaaya over lunch. The universe's cheeky—perhaps tacky provocation with the Kismi toffee bar; yet, something anchored me to this emptiness—something that I could not shake.

'Slices of experience.' The monk's words echoed in my ears.

It was an interesting concept that he had expressed in the sense of a digital camera. To someone like me who had entire hard drives full of photos, this was a relevant analogy.

I stopped walking and looked over the valley. The half-moon lit up a monochrome landscape before me. The mystique, drama, and romance of a black and white photograph hit me from the scene. I felt the cold breeze—the breath of ice from the higher peaks that were still covered with snow. The fragrance of pine freed by the sun during the day and that now floated gently into my consciousness.

I finally realised what Bhikshu Dechen meant about *slices of experience*.

I finally realised what Lama Phuntsok meant about being *Present*. During the first day of the workshop, I remember him going on and on about '*Presence* and *Awareness*'. It seemed to me that he was just stating the same thing in different words. But no. They're two completely different things. And words can't explain them perfectly.

I sat there in the moonlight, being '*Present*'—for perhaps the first time in my life.

Chapter 7

It was nearly noon when I awoke. The events of the previous day seemed like a dream—but clearly, they weren't—a Kismi toffee bar and Chaaya's hairband lay on my bedside table.

I walked to the dining room and asked Som to make me a cup of coffee. I sat on the rear lawn, overlooking the valley—now in full colour with resplendent greens and the bright blue sky. It seemed as if it was the first day of a new life. Once I finished my coffee, I took the Nikomat and walked down to Baxterpur town.

The Nikomat has no autofocus. Nor does it have auto exposure. You need to spin the focus ring on the lens to get a sharp image. You need to get your exposure right and adjust the shutter speed ring on the camera to balance a needle between two brackets. If you don't get this right, your pictures come out either too dark or too bright. Certainly, much slower than shooting with the Fuji, but not as hard as I imagined. The Nikon 50mm F/2 lens was a real treat—the focus ring slid so smoothly that you could work it with a fingertip.

I took pictures of trees, the valley, old gateposts, and three young monks walking together. It was only when I pressed the shutter button on that one that I realised what shooting black and white meant—the vermillion robes, the brown eyes, the shades of sunburn—all reduced to shades of grey. But well!

I didn't even realise how quickly I finished the roll.

Chaaya spent Thursday with me. We had breakfast together, made love until noon, and spent time talking about life in general.

'What's your daughter's name?'

'Srishti.'

'Nice name. Do you see her often?'

'No. I haven't seen her for two years.'

'Why? Because you don't want to?'

'No. Because she's in Canada and the Delhi police has my passport.'

'What? Why?' For the first time since we met, I felt her draw away.

I sighed.

'My wife is a Canadian citizen—born in Delhi though. When she left me, she filed a domestic violence complaint against me and used it as a supporting document to get an emergency passport for Srishti. The two of them left by diplomatic transport—while I was in judicial remand.'

'Seriously? Does that actually happen?'

'Well, it happened to me. She didn't appear in court several times so the judge granted bail, but I won't get my passport back until the case itself has been closed.'

'Do you miss her?'

I looked at Bunky. 'What do you think?'

'I don't know—you tell me. Some men would appreciate a new lease of freedom—travel the country with a camera, seduce the Guest Relations Managers of hotels where they stay…'

Tears welled up in my eyes. 'Not me.'

'Sorry. That was mean.'

'No, it's alright. But I do miss Srishti. She's out there somewhere—three years old now—probably learning to draw letters of the alphabet—doing Paw Patrol jigsaw puzzles—maybe holding full conversations. But in my head, she's still a one-year-old baby—who sings '*Wheels of The Bus*' and dances the 'Macarena'.'

'The Macarena? In 2019? Seriously?'

'Oh yeah. She could also do the Ketchup Song dance.'

Chaaya laughed.

The day passed in the languid indolence that had defined my life since I sold Linguintel.

On Saturday morning, Hiroto's helicopter flew over Hillcrest on the way to the Baxter Lodge. Chaaya phoned on his behalf asking me to dinner. I was intrigued. The last time we met, there was that really weird trip—the Boadicea lily tea. I wondered what this visit held.

When I entered Hiroto's suite that evening, the first thing I saw was Adachi and Hiroto making more of the Boadicea yak butter tea. I followed his precise movements just as I did the other evening. By the time Bushida served me, I was looking forward to the trip. When I sipped my cup, the familiar warmth and fragrance of the drink enveloped me—I looked forward to the expansion once the drink took hold.

My body started pulsing—as if every cell in my body was expanding and contracting in step with my heartbeat. I heard a sigh. Chaaya had her head back, cheeks flushed, a soft smile played on her lips—she was obviously off in another realm. The world around me began to colour—the pulsing eased, and I slipped into the golden blackness.

Exhilaration.

The moment that the doctor handed Srishti to me—mere minutes after she was born. The first time she called me '*baba*'. That time she first stood up—reaching for the New York City snow globe in my living room. Those moments when her spontaneous laughter would just trill through our apartment.

That moment when Sameera agreed to our first date.

The first time I kissed her. That moment when she agreed to marry me.

That moment in my college hostel—when returning

from a smoke break, realising the meagre processing power of my Pentium III computer was actually able to run the language analytics that I had designed—the computer program that became Linguintel.

The other night—standing over the moonlit valley—the cold breeze blowing with the fragrance of Guerlain Shalimar. The cold turning to warmth—the warmth of Chaaya's body in my arms. Her lips on mine, her hair caressing my face and chest, our bodies moving together—inching towards that explosion of passion and sensation, that split second of perfect calm—before we were pulled back into our pulsing, entwined bodies. Then pulled back into the world—a mundane pall over an intricate arcana—with that golden shutter in the Dwidala Camera Shop at its centre.

Bunky floated into sight. Just like the last time, he was huge—his face ten feet wide. The monk sat on his head, the Nikomat on his lap. Neither of them spoke. The monk smiled at me and nodded gently.

Bunky swirled off into the darkness taking the monk with him.

The trip ended gently.

I looked around me. Everybody seemed to have come down from a pleasant trip—flushed, perspiring slightly, but in good humour. I was relieved that I didn't throw up like last time.

We moved to the open kitchen, where the ingredients

were laid out for dinner. Adachi and Hiroto began making sushi. This was weird, but also pleasant. I liked Hiroto's style. It was a different way of eating—when you cook as a group, things feel different. I no longer felt in awe of Hiroto—the multibillionaire investor. I felt a kinship with Bushida who had taught me to fry tempura the last time I was here. In stark contrast to Akshay Bhalla's indulgent, hotel-like mansion on the outskirts of New Delhi—complete with liveried staff and a monogrammed dinner service.

Yes, perhaps I should have sold Linguintel to Sogacorp.

Adachi placed an entire makizushi roll before Hiroto. He pulled out a santoku knife and cut it into six pieces—two pieces each for Chaaya, Bushida, and me. I knew enough to eat sushi with my fingers. I sipped the excellent sake and took in the 'look' of this sushi. It looked very professional—tight, well cut.

Hiroto caught my eye. 'Well?'

I put the sushi in my mouth. Fantastic. The salmon, shrimp, and wait—Basmati rice?

'Basmati rice?' I asked Hiroto.

Hiroto smiled.

I turned to Chaaya. 'Basmati rice?'

'Yes. I love it,' said Hiroto, 'I just love the flavour—it's just so…it seeps down to your soul. It's the finest food on the planet. If the Japanese had known it three hundred years ago, we'd be growing it ourselves.'

'How do you get it to stick?'

'Just don't wash it—take it right out of the bag and boil it.'

I tried the second piece. Yes, it was amazing.

'Our turn,' Bushida said to me.

Makizushi isn't hard. I wonder why people think it's fancy.

You take a bamboo mat, spread a sheet of seaweed over it, spread a light layer of rice, then the stuffings—salmon, finely chopped pickled spring onions, and some crab. Next you roll the mat tight, while you moisten the edge of the seaweed sheet to help it seal. I don't think Bushida trusted me with the knife—he cut it himself—first into half, next the two halves into three pieces each.

I was enthused. We made another round before Hiroto and Chaaya took over.

A few rounds later, Adachi and Bushida retreated to one of the rooms in the suite. Chaaya left too, telling me that I could sleep in room 23, if needed.

That left Hiroto and me, alone, with a fresh bottle of Sudo Honke.

'Tell me about Linguintel.'

'It's in the past.'

'Indulge me.' He filled up my sake cup until it overflowed.

'Linguintel. It started when I was in college.

'A typical degree mill—one of the thousands that

sprang up in southern India in the 1990s. Everything was mediocre—the college, teachers, infrastructure. Despite spending four years preparing for the IIT entrance exams, I had failed. But with the intense mathematics and science learning needed for the exam preparations—I could breeze through the engineering syllabus.'

'I see. I've heard about these colleges,' Hiroto said.

'This classmate of mine—Puran, a soft-spoken, really smart boy from Jhansi—had calculus and physics theory at his fingertips. He would even help the third-year boys with their assignments. But Puran was sensitive—he couldn't stand profanity; even cigarette smoke would make him nauseous. It didn't help that he was somewhat effeminate—slender build—nearly hairless face, even at 18.

Puran stood first in the university exams in the first year. Everyone knew he deserved it. The teachers were proud. The management even gave him a fee waiver. Two months into the second year, stories started to swirl. Someone was putting out a weekly email titled '*Adventures of Puran*'. The email contained a four or five panel comic strip which depicted him engaging in graphic homosexual acts with members of the college's service staff and other solitary students. The college took this seriously, but in those days, there was no concept of Cyber Crime or online harassment.'

'That sounds awful.' Hiroto seemed genuinely horrified.

'He didn't really bother about it initially, but it soon

started to get to him. People started joking about it, joking turned to taunting…

'One day, in tears, he told me that there should be a way to tell who was writing these—there should be something in the style of his writing—vocabulary, choice of words, sentence structure, that would tie to the individual based on his background, education, ethnicity—you know, what we would call Machine Learning basics today. But this was 1999. We didn't have Python, data science, or stuff like that to work on what Puran called '*Linguistic Intelligence*'.

'That night, Puran hung himself.

'His death hit everyone. I don't know if the person who was writing these stories actually meant to do him harm. Puran wasn't the demonstrative type—no outbursts—no talking back. He would just shake his head and move on. He had no enemies. Impossible to dislike. I needed to find the person who caused this.

'Three months later, while on a trip to Bangalore, I found a book on solving complex analytical problems using Neural Networks in C++ at a second-hand book shop. I worked on a program nights and weekends for a year, and created a system—basically, you could put in a subject profile—attributes linked to an individual—education level, mother tongue, other languages spoken, place of birth—up to 256 attributes to each subject. Along with that subject profile, you could also upload their original writing. By the time you get a few thousand profiles in the system, you could in principle—upload a piece of text, and the system would spit out a set of attributes on a scale—I called it a conviction scale—that you could use to get an idea of the person who may have written it. It would say something like 80% chance native Hindi speaker; 60% chance also speaks English and Tamil; 96.5% chance educated in the English language until the high school level; and so forth.

'Though a real shithole in many ways, our college was a bit ahead of its time in one respect. As a part of its marketing spiel and to justify the one-million-rupee donation they demanded to admit students to engineering courses, they gave every student a PC connected to the college network. They also had a mandatory Communicative English paper each term that was beyond the prescribed academic requirements for the course. The college network was a crappy Novell Netware system that could be hacked by a child. I hacked it. I logged on to the English department's server and downloaded all the CE papers submitted to the college. I manually entered subject attributes for over three thousand students. Every six months, I would update the database with CE papers. I had an old Pentium III computer that took four weeks of non-stop operation to process the data. The complete process never ran. The power would fail, the system would overheat, something would stop, but I kept the database working.

'I finished college and graduated with a good enough

score. I got a job at a call centre in Bangalore. I shared an apartment in a gated community with four others. I needed that apartment because it was the only way to have reliable power supply to let the program run. It took me two years of saving up half my take-home pay to buy a second-hand server system. It was hardly special—a Xeon 2.4, but it was good enough. The system would process, and give me some pointers, but never anything granular enough. The problem is, the dataset from the college was quite alike. Eighty per cent of the students were from southern India, multilingual, coming from similar backgrounds. So, I built another system to scan the blogs that were being put up by people on GeoCities and Blogspot. Again, I would fill out the attributes from what I could gather from their biography pages, and the system would check blogs every 30 days for updates. In five years, I had over thirty thousand author profiles in the system and I had two data entry operators working on adding new profiles each day.'

Hiroto refilled my glass. 'And you did all of this while working full time?'

'Working an entry level job at an IT Services company in India is pretty tame. You get in there, do your nine hours—twelve hours actually, because you have no rights—and nobody complains. As long as you have no ambitions of being promoted and can swallow your ego when you're being treated like shit, you can just coast along and rack up 10% pay hikes each year. I did make one job change—200% pay hike and I moved to Gurgaon.'

'What about life?'

'I had no life. For 10 years, I had no life. It was work, the server, saving up for a bigger system to do more churning. I had a few friends I would go out with once a month or so—never really had a girlfriend. I lost my virginity on my thirtieth birthday to the woman I would marry six months later.

'The pay hike was good for Linguintel. Gurgaon was good too. I met other tech entrepreneurs, managed to get some VC funding, and finally had a small office and data centre of my own. The operation began to grow; we began to offer a use case for our technology in detecting academic plagiarism.

'Then in 2018 an anonymous letter appeared in the *New York Times*. This letter was critical of President Trump and obviously caused a major uproar. An Israeli company asked for our help to identify the whistleblower. We gave them a profile. The next day, Shaybee came knocking.'

'What about life?'

'Completely fucked. Wife took off, taking my daughter along. I found myself with three million dollars and an empty life.'

'Did you find the person who wrote the *Adventures of Puran?*'

I didn't have an answer for him.

He understood.

We sat there for another hour or so, sipping sake in silence. The emptiness inside me returned. The silence made it worse. I couldn't sit there anymore.

'Thank you for the lovely evening. I think I should go.'

'Come and see me when you're back in Delhi. I want to talk about Linguintel's future.'

Sake fucking creeps up on you. They serve it cold, it's sweetish—no taste of alcohol. So, at the end of the day, if you've been sipping it for a few hours, especially the good stuff that Hiroto and his ninjas have been splashing around—you're quite drunk. It may have been better to sleep in 23, as Chaaya suggested, but I decided to head back to Hillcrest.

That's the good thing about being drunk in the mountains. You can be as disgracefully soused as you like, and there won't be any witnesses. I staggered back home and reached the crest of the hill that Hillcrest was ostensibly named after. Dawn was breaking, but the landscape wasn't coloured yet. The emptiness inside was gnawing. I felt like screaming.

So why did I fail Puran?

I don't know. Does one get so immersed in the minutiae of life that one loses sight of what was important? But how does one lose sight of vengeance?

But why did I want to find the person who wrote the *Adventures of Puran?* Did I want to kill him? I could kill him now if I found him. You could put a hit out on someone in Gurgaon for ten million rupees. Cheaper in other parts of the country. But I didn't want to kill him. I don't remember ever thinking of that. Did I just want to prove that I was smart enough to do it? I don't know. The concept of Linguintel was perhaps the last thing that Puran had told me about. Even the name—Linguintel—was a contraction of Linguistic Intelligence—the words that Puran had used.

I had to meet the only person I knew who would have an answer.

'Good timing!' the monk said rapping the shutter.

As soon as we sat down, the server walked into the shop with lunch—pork momos and a heavy soup for me. Instead of the Canada Dry, he brought a glass jug full of salted lime juice. A Snickers bar was on the tray. These lunches weren't a surprise anymore.

'Why do we lose sight of things?'

His spoon paused mid-air for a second, but continued its trajectory. He didn't immediately answer. I took a couple of sips of the soup—the salt and fat hit my tongue and I felt my energy return. I used chopsticks to dip the corner of one of the momos in chilli sauce and stuck it in my mouth.

'Everyone on earth is lost. That's what samsara is about—layers of suffering that cause people to lose their way. Why is it that every faith talks about some sort of salvation? A destiny beyond that of this earth.'

'Why did I lose my way?'

'Did you have one to begin with?'

'I did.'

'You have just one journey—that which begins within your mother's body and ends in dust. Everything else is just a distraction. You know what we believe—we have been through this before—each one of us. Hundreds, maybe thousands of births. Passing through samsara hoping to be one with eternity. There are layers to samsara—sometimes we find our way and elevate, but more often we lose our way and descend. It's easy for the earthworm to ascend. You eat mud and expel it, and when you die, you enter a higher life. The human form is the most dangerous in that sense you have the ego, a society that works against you in every way imaginable throwing money, sex, power, fame, everything in your way to distract you, and the higher you rise in this world, the harder it is to focus on your celestial journey.'

'Right.'

'Think about Shakyamuni. The Buddha. In today's world, he would be laughed at—considered a fool—for renouncing a kingdom, wealth, power, property. He would be dishonoured—a man who abandoned his wife and infant child to go on a quest—something that no one understood.'

'True.'

'Teachers such as Phuntsok speak these truths every day, many listen, very few find the courage to follow.'

'It's brave to be a monk.'

'Not really. It was easy for me. I'm not from a wealthy family—being a novitiate meant that my father had one less mouth to feed. The Sangha was good for me, and I've found my place. Now you—you have a job that could pay for an entire Fujifilm kit. How easy will it be for you to leave it all behind? Don't answer.'

We ate in silence for a few minutes.

'You know, that 50mm that you have—they call it a normal lens. That's because its angle of view—the amount of a scene that it captures—is very similar to what the human eye sees. The human eye sees only a portion of what exists—once you add the other senses—hearing, smell, touch, taste, they're all equally blinkered—you perceive only part of the world around you. Even a minor expansion is a stretch.'

'I have a couple of wide angles for the Fuji.'

'Have you ever really used them?'

I took a long swig of the salty lemon juice. My head was clearing.

'No, not really. I don't think I've ever really used my Fuji gear.'

'Sometimes it helps to step back a bit. See something a little wider.'

We finished our meal. When I was getting ready to

leave, the monk went to one of the red boxes and pulled out a lens.

'This is a 35mm lens. It's just a little wider than normal. See how this works for you.'

'I have nothing to trade in today, so you'll just have to take cash.'

The monk smiled. 'Borrow it. If you like it, we'll work something out.'

'Do you ever take cash? How do you keep this place running?'

'I'm a Bhikshu. The generosity of my fellow creatures provides everything I need.'

I walked back to Hillcrest munching on the snickers bar. The monk was right. Samsara is a living breathing quagmire that reaches out with gooey tendrils and pulls you back in. Perhaps this is why one needs lifetimes—many of them—with each cycle of birth and death taking one perhaps an inch towards freedom of the soul.

I reached Hillcrest and asked Som for a cup of tea. A few minutes later, he brought me a cup of the super sweet beverage. I found the joint that Chaaya had given me the day we found the Boadicea lily.

I lit it up.

Moments of great clarity are often followed by moments of greater anxiety. It's almost as if there are parts of your psyche that thrive on disorder and anguish. Lying there on the rear lawn, I wondered about everything that had happened in the past few weeks. I needed to do something. I needed to get Srishti back. I needed to find the author of the *Adventures of Puran.*

I needed to return to Delhi.

OOO

Chapter 8

I started with making space.

I began to get rid of stuff. Sameera's clothes—all of them. I packed them into large garbage bags and turned them over to a charity. I kept all of Srishti's stuff though. I called a professional cleaning service to deep clean the entire flat.

I called my lawyers—both the criminal lawyer handling my case—and the family lawyer, who had advised me on the divorce and custody matter. I set up appointments for the next day.

The house-cleaning team had used floor cleaners that smelt faintly of lemon. It was a nice touch—it wiped out the heavy smell of camphor and sandalwood from the incense sticks that Sameera used to light—smells that lingered in this home even two years after she had left.

The flat was still too cluttered. Full of things that I had bought to fill the void in my life left by Linguintel's sale and Sameera's desertion—video game consoles, DVD movies, a ukulele bought for me by a Tinder date, who lasted a month. I moved everything into one of the bedrooms—filled the cupboards, stacked some things on the bed, and then locked the door.

It felt good. I remembered reading an utterly forgettable airport paperback—something about getting rid of things that don't spark happiness or some such dumb shit. Maybe there was some truth to that. The best part is, you don't even have to get rid of those things, but just lock them in a room—out of sight—just like trauma.

I checked on my car. Despite not using it for a year, it started the moment I reconnected the battery. God Bless Toyota. I dropped it off at the service centre.

I spent the evening at a brewery that was walking distance from the apartment. I missed the silence of Hillcrest Cottage. Gurgaon's thick, smoky air was getting to me. The noisy, jampacked bar hurt my senses. I longed to be back at Baxterpur, spending time with Chaaya or lunching with the monk. But I did have these things to do. It's easy to let the hard parts of life fester—even if you're one of those *'get out there and get it done'* types.

The criminal lawyer said we had to wait for the next court date to file a petition to retrieve my travel documents and another to 'quash' Sameera's police report. He'd been saying the same thing for the past two years. The court system was too complicated for a mere engineer to understand. The family lawyer said material progress would only be possible once the criminal charges were resolved. Back to square one.

I called Gautam K Hejamady.

'Hey, where are you boss? Three years almost up!' came Hejamady's deep baritone. No 'hi', no 'hello'—it was over a year since we last spoke.

'Just hanging around man. What's up with you?'

'Just waiting for the three years to finish and for Shaybee to buy my shares, and then at your feet for the next venture.'

That made me laugh. 'You're fucking optimistic.'

'Boss, we started by eating Top Ramen in a slum in Bangalore and ended up drinking 70-year-old whiskey with Akshay Bhalla. Anything is possible.'

'Time for a drink?'

'Where?'

'Same place.'

'Twenty minutes boss.' He hung up.

Hejamady, or GK as we all called him, was Linguintel's first employee. When I was looking for a data entry operator, it was really hard to find someone who would stick around. No one lasted more than a week. I admit, I was a little intense in those days—I'd rain hell if someone made a mistake.

I met GK during my Bangalore days. He worked as a waiter at a dive I frequented on Saturday nights. He was meticulous, attentive—a people's person. One night after I saw him deal with a particularly aggressive drunk, I asked him if he wanted an office job. GK spoke decent English and was a voracious reader. His colleagues called him GK not for his initials, but for his 'general knowledge'—the hoard of trivia in his skull that bourgeois schools' treasure.

It wasn't much of an office job. GK worked out of his shared flat, but he had a laptop—a real status symbol, the mark of having an 'important' job in 2006. It grew from there. I was able to pay him increments and gave him a big bump when I moved to Gurgaon. He was smart—apart from pulling 12-hour data entry shifts for me, he spent time studying. By the time my first round of funding came in, I was able to name him my Head of Systems and give him equity. Because of his technical role, Shaybee gave him only a partial exit in the acquisition—the bulk of his equity would be bought out only after three years with the company.

GK walked into the pub exactly twenty minutes after he hung up. He spotted me and walked over. We hugged, and he hopped on to the bar stool next to me. He put an iPhone and an Audi fob on the bar. I picked it up.

'Audi, wow! Which one?'

'A6 boss. 2014 model. Third owner.'

'How many Kms?'

'Eighty thousand.'

'Still brand new.'

He smiled with a twinkle in his eye 'Yes boss, gave it a proper service and it's just like new.'

I caught up on the Linguintel gossip—all of my original team was still there—obviously, stuck with the same buyout clause. GK said everyone was desperate to leave—the CEO Shaybee had installed had been treating them badly. They had some projects, talk of a sale, but nothing major had come through—either by way of projects or acquisitions.

The evening wore on, and we were three pitchers of beer down—bathed in the glow of being happily tipsy. The gossip ended, and for fifteen minutes we sat in each other's presence, looking into our beer. Our entire history played through my head, and I looked up at him and smiled. He smiled back at me—I think he had been playing his memory reel too.

'I need access to the centre node.'

His smile faded.

'I thought you had forgotten about that boss.'

'Not forgotten GK, things got in the way. But now I need to finish it.'

'Why now? When the VC money came, you forgot all about it. Now you're sitting here with twenty-five crores, without a life, without a wife, and looking for the old projects to finish'

'Nonsense.'

Tears appeared at the corner of his eyes.

'It was a night like this—remember? We were drinking at *The Night Watchman* and you told me about Puran. Then it was another night like this, when we celebrated the VC money at 4S. You started with this but then Sameera told you to shut up about the sad story and celebrate the funding. You didn't open your mouth that whole evening. You drank eight full bottles of KF Strong and fell unconscious. Yashodhan and I had to carry you home. You never spoke about Puran after that.'

That last sentence stung like a slap. That's certainly not the way I remembered it.

'I need access to the centre node.'

He sat silent for five minutes.

'Let's meet at the Westin for breakfast tomorrow. Nine a.m.'

He slid off the bar stool.

I picked up his car keys. 'Take an Uber.'

'Oh, come on boss—It's hardly…'

'Take a fucking Uber. Tomorrow. Nine. Westin I'll be there.'

I walked home. Sobering up after that much beer is easy—chug a litre of water, cold shower, chug another litre of water, wait until you piss three times, and then go to bed.

The next morning, GK walked into the Westin at nine sharp.

We served ourselves from the breakfast buffet and sat at a corner table.

'How was your night?' I asked.

'I haven't drunk like that for long time.' He smiled. 'But I'm okay.'

'So, the centre node.'

'Not possible.'

'Why?'

'There's a new system; we don't have our own datacentre now. We ported Linguintel to Amazon Web Services to save the server cost when we started analysing social media.'

'You're analysing social media now?'

'The way we used to scan blogs for patterns, we're now scanning Facebook, voice feeds from YouTube videos, about 120 social media sources in 43 languages.'

Well, fuck—this was way beyond what I thought they could do.

'So now it is running on AWS, and because each query has cost, every server entry gets tracked. You cannot log in. I can run a query, but there has to be a reason.'

'How're you going to do it?'

'We're always pitching to investors—I'm going to run stress test of the system to tune the algorithms. That way I would be run the comparison of the *Adventures of Puran* against whole database. This time, I'll able to run all 23 episodes against the dataset. It will cost Linguintel about twenty-k dollars in AWS cost.'

'Can you do it safely?'

'Yes. But max to max I can be fired—who cares.'

'What are you saying?'

'They can't do anything more.'

'Don't risk your buyback, man.'

'Fuck the buyback boss. That's how Shaybee controls people. Me and Yash and Kirti and Anshika don't care about the buyback. I will say it on his face one day. Bhalla will shit in his pants.'

That evening, Sunny called.

Of all of Sameera's relatives, I got along best with Sunny, her cousin. About my age, he too was an entrepreneur. Every couple of months, we met for drinks. Once Sameera took off and the whole family came to know of it—contact ended.

We spoke for about half an hour, cautiously talking around the elephant in the room. As we were about to end the conversation, he told me he had called because Sameera and Srishti were coming to India to attend a wedding. He was unsure why he was telling me—thought I should know.

I drove up to Baxterpur on Wednesday.

Chaaya came to Hillcrest to spend Thursday with me. We went for a long walk in the spring sun, cameras in hand. She would kneel now and then to photograph something by the path. I took mindless landscapes with my 35mm lens. We returned to Hillcrest for lunch.

'You're unusually silent,' she said.

'Nothing really. Life seemed to kick off when I went to Gurgaon.'

'Did you meet Hiroto?'

'No. I was just busy with my own stuff. Got my house ready, caught up on some old business, met some old friends, my lawyers.'

'And?'

'Sameera's cousin called me. Sameera and Srishti are coming to India next month for a wedding.'

'What did the lawyers say?'

'Nothing can be done unless the criminal cases are dealt with. I don't even know if I should try to see Srishti at her grandparents' home.'

'Who's getting married?'

'Her cousin Suhani. She runs the fashion label—Suhani G. She's marrying some Bombay-based investment banker. Seems it will be a fancy affair—they're having the reception at the Imperial Hotel, New Delhi.'

'Suhani Gulati? Oh my…I wouldn't expect anything less than the Imperial.'

'You know her?'

'Well, I know of her. She's a regular in the Delhi jet set.'

My phone rang. The screen flashed the name of the head of the police station, where the case against me had been filed.

'Hello?'

'Come to the station,' the man said in Hindi.

'Sir, I am out of town. Is there a problem?'

'A problem? You fucker—you are an accused in a

domestic violence case, a wanted criminal—and you're asking me if there is a problem?' Where are you?'

'I'm in Uttarakhand. Baxterpur.'

'Having fun with some chick?'

'No sir. I just came here to trek in the mountains. I'll return tomorrow. Can I come and meet you at 5 pm?'

'Day after tomorrow at 8 am. Don't be late.'

I texted my criminal lawyer and returned to lunch.

'Delhi Police and their elevated people skills,' I muttered.

'Should I come back to Delhi with you?' she asked, visibly concerned.

'No. What would you do there? The weather is already taking a turn for the worse.'

'Well, it's been a while since I've visited Delhi. I could use a few days in the city.'

'What about the lodge?'

'The staff will manage. It won't be a problem.'

In my head, I congratulated myself for cleaning up the apartment.

The drive to Delhi was fun. Chaaya had an eclectic taste in music. Her playlist included Duran Duran, Oasis, Simon & Garfunkel, Maroon 5, Imagine Dragons, and Coldplay. She had packed a food hamper from Baxter Lodge that we devoured over two rest breaks. I felt an energy that I've never felt. We were on the national highway and I was swerving and skidding like the maniac drivers I used to swear at just a month earlier. We blew into Delhi at 120 kilometres an hour to Adam Levine belting out 'Animals'.

We stopped at a supermarket near the apartment and stocked up on supplies. The energy from the trip endured. Despite the long drive, I felt energetic, alive—maybe this is what love feels like.

We showered, cooked a Gnocchi and pesto dinner that we washed down with an entire bottle of an Indian Sauvignon Blanc. Yes, I know. Fuck you.

The next morning, I woke up at five to get ready. We decided to drive to the police station—Chaaya would keep the car and wait for me at a nearby coffee shop.

We reached the police station at 7.45 am. Come 8 am, the officer wasn't there. I phoned him at 8.15 am. He called me a bastard, insulted me with another reference to being a criminal, and told me to wait. I waited.

Chaaya called at noon.

'Hey, what's up?'

'No sign of him. I phoned him—the usual shit.'

'Oh damn. I'm calling a friend. He will meet you at the police station.'

'Who?'

'A lawyer friend.'

'I have a lawyer.'

'This one is better.'

An hour later, there was a bit of a flurry at the entrance

of the police station. A familiar looking elderly man in a light grey linen suit walked in and scanned the chaotic room. His eyes caught mine and he walked to me.

'Harish Arya?'

I rose to my feet instinctively. 'Yes.'

He handed me his card.

It was a plain white card—elegant ivory stock with plain black copperplate lettering.

K N Darbari.

(A landline number.)

(An address on Amrita Sher Gill Road—the most exclusive residential street in India.)

Then it clicked. I had seen him on Television shows—on a World Economic Forum broadcast even.

We shook hands. I was at a loss for words.

'Chaaya Singh said you might need some help.'

'Yes, Mr Darbari—I'm honoured. Thank you for coming.'

I had heard gossip that Darbari has a base fee of ten million rupees. I wondered how much this was going to set me back.

'Who is this person you are here to meet?'

'Inspector BS Atwal.'

'Excuse me. I need to make a phone call.'

'That's alright.'

He pulled out a pushbutton cell phone from an inside pocket and stepped away. A minute later, he sat down beside me.

'I know you have been waiting for a while—please bear with this for another hour.'

A few minutes later, a police constable brought us two cups of tea. Darbari helped himself to the tea. I declined.

Ten minutes later, a sweating Inspector Atwal rushed into the police station. Without a word, he motioned to his office and we followed him.

'Please, please sit.' Atwal motioned to the chairs—a refreshing change from his past behaviour with me.

Darbari made himself comfortable. 'So, Inspector Atwal. Why do you need to see my client? There's no charge sheet, and there's no open summons.'

'Sir, just a routine follow-up with him about the complaint. The case is still open.'

'Atwal, my client was enjoying a vacation in Uttarakhand yesterday. You summoned him here to the station today and kept him waiting for six hours now. You have not been able to file a chargesheet for two years. I will be moving to have the FIR quashed. So, what do you need to ask him about this case that you haven't asked him in two years?'

Atwal was silent for about ten seconds.

'Sir actually…' his tone was one of anxious contrition. 'His wife's father got in touch with me. She and the child are coming back to India next month. He wanted me to warn him not to make any trouble.'

'Anything else?' Darbari asked.

'No. That is it sir. Sorry for the delay. There was a murder at seven in the morning, that's why I was late.'

'Okay. Let's go. Come on Harish.'

Darbari walked me to a shiny white Volkswagen Polo parked on the street outside the police station.

'Thank you so much, Mr Darbari. We need to...'

'Let's proceed with your lunch plans—I will be intruding, but I think I have earned it.'

'Of course.' I got into the car. 'There's still the matter of your fee.'

'Don't worry about that, Harish. Chaaya's a close friend's daughter. I will get this FIR quashed. If you want to retain me, we'll work out a fee—and no, I don't charge a crore just to open my mouth.'

Darbari drove to the mall where Chaaya was waiting for us.

We had a long lunch that drew into teatime. Darbari and Chaaya were obviously close. Their conversation, often conspiratorial, had references to her schooling at one of those boarding schools in the hills, and their mutual acquaintances in the Delhi jet set.

When I was paying the bill Darbari turned to me.

'I was serious about getting the FIR quashed. Meet me with your counsel.'

'Sure.'

For most of that week Chaaya split her time between my apartment and her parents' home. The next Thursday, I drove her back to Baxterpur. When I was driving back to Gurgaon, Hiroto texted asking to meet.

Chapter 9

Hiroto's pied-e-terre was in the heart of New Delhi—on the second floor of a lovely art-deco-style building with red sandstone cladding. Homes on the street had nameplates announcing the official residences of consuls, ambassadors, and diplomatic attaches.

The inside of the home was beautiful. It seemed as if the entire flat had been gutted and redone in a minimalistic Japanese style with clean straight lines. The decor was elegant—white walls, window drapes with tones of beige and nearly indiscernible gold edges, and gorgeous Japanese furniture. The centrepiece was a wooden display frame with six Samurai swords—three pairs of short and long swords—in lustrous black lacquer scabbards with silk tassels.

We ate dinner in his signature style—the four of us took turns making sushi and then Bushida and Adachi put together ramen bowls as the main course. After dinner, Adachi and Bushida retired to their rooms, leaving Hiroto, me, and a bottle of Sudo Honke.

'Nice place,' I said to break the silence.

'Thank you,' he said. 'I spend a lot of time in India these days. I dislike Bombay—but here, I'm close to my lawyers and a two-hour chopper ride to Baxterpur.'

My eyes wandered to the swords. 'I guessed right—Adachi and Bushida are ninjas.'

Hiroto laughed. 'They'd be offended at the suggestion—calling someone a ninja isn't really a compliment in Japan. But by your reasoning, what does that make me?'

'A *taikun*, I guess.'

Hiroto smiled. 'Ninjas and Samurai in Japan—Knights, Earls, and Squires in Europe—isn't it amusing how we romanticise brutish power structures? The Daimyo system was replaced in the 1860s by Kazoku—just another name for the same class hierarchy, abolished again in 1947. I spent eight years at Eton and ten at Oxford—same thing. All those Lords and Knights—a hierarchy of violence—now dressed in silly striped pants, colour coded by their waistcoats.'

'Eton and Oxford—it could be argued that you come from the same hierarchy of violence.'

'Yes. I do. My great-great grandfather was a Daimyo. During the Meiji restoration it became clear to him that the order was going to change. He sent his Samurai to Europe to study—and to India, Malacca, and Suez to work. By the Second World War we were already a global banking and mercantile conglomerate with offices in Calcutta, Cochin, Malacca, London, Suez, Casablanca—even New York.'

'The order never changes.'

'Oh, the order did! Most of the so-called noble houses in Japan were reduced to penury by the early 20th century. Even their pride in their military history hit the dust after the Second World War—hundreds of Japanese military officers claiming noble blood died by Seppuku—ritual suicide—the day Japan surrendered. The old order ended.'

'Really?'

'A few evolved. Adachi and Bushida are descendants of ancient Samurai clans. Their grandfathers, who worked for my great-grandfather, embraced the access that their privilege gave them much before the Second World War. Sogacorp is a Han—a fiefdom—my clan and two Samurai families getting on like the good old days.'

'I'm surprised you don't see the contradiction in that. The old order survives. You're still here, still wealthy…'

'And powerful,' he interjected, 'and with the ability—though not necessarily the appetite—for violence.'

'So, what's changed?'

'Values.'

An involuntary bellow of mirth forced a mist of sake through my nose and mouth. I choked laughing—and it took me the better part of a minute to recover. I eventually used a tactic that our paediatrician taught Srishti—you stretch your arms above your head and cough. Even for an adult, it works well enough—worth looking silly for ten seconds. Hiroto watched in silence as I composed myself. He didn't seem annoyed or insulted.

'It's only your power and privilege that enables you to speak of values,' I said.

'You're right. And that's why a change in values is important. Societies realign their values all the time. I'll speak of Japan again—the Meiji Restoration happened because Emperor Meiji realised that a tenuous confederacy of temperamental warlords stood no chance against gunpowder. Again, Hirohito's surrender in 1945 realigned the empire's values—from a divine duty to the emperor to accepting and enduring the humiliation of defeat.'

'What about the Soga family's values?'

'We were just swept along. Our warehouses were taken over, our vessels impounded due to our participation in the war effort. Luckily, the family estate in Nara was too far away to be strategically significant to MacArthur. We were left with just our men and some land. In 1949, seventy-four of our people from around the world—clerks, accountants, traders from our businesses—met in Nara. We put together all the money that had been saved from seizure. People had come to Japan with promissory notes and British pounds sewn into their coats, gemstones and gold coins hidden in furniture and what not. My grandfather put it all together and started three companies. Today, Sogacorp owns over four hundred companies—only six are listed on a stock exchange. I'm just trying to run the Han—the fief—trying to keep everyone safe, comfortable, provided for.'

'Doing what?'

'Well, you know of Sogacorp for a handful of investments in spheres where boastfulness is the norm—but nearly all of our money goes to quiet businesses that—pardon the cliche—make the world a better place.'

'Of course.'

'Let me explain. I must. Capitalism simplifies things. Not always for the good—but it reduces us all—you, me, Adachi, Bushida, Chaaya—seven billion Homo sapiens of this planet. Each one of us are complex beings—physical, emotional, psychological, sexual, spiritual—we exist in dimensions that we may not even be aware of. These parts need to be gratified, tended, nurtured, endured. But capitalism—reduces all of us to a simple entity—a number—an economic entity. Hiroto Soga—forty-three billion dollars according to *Forbes*. Harish Arya—three million dollars from the Linguintel sale. Akshay Bhalla—three billion dollars from the notional value of the twenty companies that Shaybee has invested in.'

'This simplicity makes it easier to work with. Ninety-nine percent of this planet is motivated by money. All their wants, desires, beliefs, ambitions, can be tied to a number—a certain amount of money. So, if you're in my situation, changing anything is just a matter of finding the right price—and paying it. That's what we have been doing for seventy years. Hirohito turned the system on its head. The Americans came in with their badly behaved soldiers and their obscene capitalists. They were all so easy to work with.'

'Was it all really that simple?'

'Not always—but mostly. The entire world was governed by one thing only—money. Integrity, compassion, loyalty, honour—all fell by the wayside. Adachi's son in London does nothing but drive a Ferrari and sleep with any woman willing to go home with him. Bushida's daughter—a US citizen—is an activist at an organization with noble motives, but a nihilistic agenda dictated by technology billionaires—gender identity, affirmative action and whatnot.'

'I could debate the merits of that agenda, but let's not go there today. Tell me—how would your buying Linguintel have made the world a better place?'

Hiroto refilled our glasses.

'The idea was amazing—the way your database was breaking down the finer points of communication. But you had it backwards. You have all this rich data on how a person's upbringing, education, and circumstances influence his communication, and you use it to determine the characteristics of text. Absurd. Imagine if you built a communication engine over that database. Hiroto writes Harish an email—but the email Harish receives uses his own style, his words. No baffling idiom, no misinterpretation of meaning or tone.'

'And a complete fucking loss of individuality, style, and personality,' I shot back instinctively.

'Mostly overrated.'

'What if I intentionally wanted to insult someone?'

'How often have you written an email to insult someone?'

'How would you monetise it?'

Hiroto laughed. 'Ah, Mo-Ho-Ne-He-Tize—the incantation of dim-witted venture capitalists. I'd licence it to social media marketing agencies, newspapers, and bloggers. I'd build a tool where you could log in and read any article in your individual style. You wouldn't judge the language or tone—whether it's written by an Oxford don, technology billionaire, or a Syrian refugee. You could market a Toyota Corolla to Puff Daddy—and it would make sense to him.'

I sat there in silence, trying to make sense of what Hiroto had just said. It was innovative—a direction that I had never considered. Of course. I was driven by revenge. I wasn't building a company—I was building a computer system to find the men who pushed my friend to suicide. Even the initial monetisation of it was to keep the project alive—I wasn't even selling it.

'Would the ability to sell a Toyota Corolla to Puff

Daddy really make this world a better place?'

'Well, think of it this way—the internet and social media have given people the ability to broadcast their views—but are those views really *understood* by the readers? One could argue that a platform that helps people understand each other—would make this world a better place. What do you think?'

I thought he made a good point.

We finished the bottle of sake, and Hiroto showed me to a room—a simple bedroom with an attached bath. I showered and went to bed.

The next morning, while driving back home, my phone rang.

'Good morning, Mr Arya, please hold for Mr Akshay Bhalla,' said a female voice.

'OK.'

'Hey Harish, how's it going?'

'Going ok, how can I help you?'

'I would like to see you for lunch—could you come to the Delhi Golf Club at 12.30?'

The arrogant bastard. 'Sorry Akshay, I have a really packed schedule today and for the next few days. Could I call you back once I've shuffled a few things around?'

'I would prefer if we could meet today. I need to clear up some things about your recent meetings with Linguintel employees.'

'Akshay, I'm driving. I'll call you back as soon

as I reach home.'

I disconnected.

I called him back as soon as I reached home and agreed to meet him at his home that night.

Dining with Akshay Bhalla is completely different from a meal with Hiroto. Bhalla is the larger-than-life private equity investor. He lives in a sprawling compound in Delhi's farmhouse district—ten acres is my guess—a large house with a uniformed staff. There's a bar with a collection of whiskies from around the world—he likes calling out bottles and telling you how rare they are. Occasionally, he'll tell you that the whiskey he has served you is a thousand dollars a sip. I don't like him—I only went because what he said sounded like a threat to GK.

The same script as the other two times I was in this house. A liveried valet took my car at the porch. Another uniformed attendant walked me into the home, where a black-clad bouncer frisked me. The attendant led me to the living room bar—an atrium large enough to be a hotel's reception. I walked around for a bit, reading the whiskey labels—guessing the pronunciation of the Irish and Scottish names in my head. The attendant and bouncer stood in a corner keeping an eagle-eye on me.

Akshay Bhalla has always been a formidable character. His public image and persona were meticulously managed to convey a sense of genteel ominousness. Even this place, red and black granite—a hideous colour scheme for a residence—illuminated by incandescent bulbs and cooled to twenty degrees Celsius, felt like an antechamber to hell.

He was a scary person to do business with too. When there were disagreements over a company's valuation, fortuitous mishaps occurred. Someone's infidelity would,escalate into a public scandal—someone would be grievously injured in a bar fight or road rage incident, or a company would lose customer information due to a data hack. It then struck me—did Bhalla have *anything* to do with Sameera taking off? I didn't really fight him on the valuation though. He named a figure—my banker did a formal valuation based on revenues and a textbook formula—and we met just short of half-way.

Bhalla walked in.

'Sorry Harish, I had a call with the Blackstone guys in NY that overshot by a bit.' He shook hands with his vice grip. 'What would you like to drink? Whiskey?'

'Whiskey works,' I said.

'What kind? I just got a new batch from an auction in Hong Kong. Some really unique stuff.'

'Nah, nothing special. Do you have anything Japanese?'

His face tightened. Ah, so he knew that Soga and I were hanging out. He turned to the attendant and asked for a bottle of Hibiki.

We walked on to the terrace where four chairs and a table were laid out. Bhalla opened a humidor placed on the table and lit a large cigar. The attendant arrived with the drinks trolley bearing a bottle of Hibiki, two crystal whiskey glasses, a crystal ice-bucket, and a shimmering crystal water bottle.

'Water and ice, right?' Bhalla asked.

'Yes please.'

The attendant made our drinks.

'Don't think I'm pompous Harish, but these glasses cost more than that bottle of whiskey.'

'Well, that's alright—for a guy who drank nothing but Kingfisher beer for the first ten years of his adult life, this is quite a luxury anyway.'

He smirked. 'Well, one could argue that for such a person, just holding one of those glasses is luxury enough.'

Akshay Bhalla wasn't scary anymore.

'Well, before you act on that…' I drained the glass and set it back on the table with a tap. I looked him in the eye. 'What did you want to speak with me about?'

'I hear that you have been meeting with Linguintel employees.'

'Not employees—just one employee—GK. But I don't see why it would bother you so much as to call me here.'

'I'm just trying to protect my investment. I'm aware that you have been meeting with the Sogacorp people. In fact, their lawyer seems to have taken up some of your legal affairs.'

'And this concerns you because?'

'We're just a short time away from the end of the

non-compete window with Linguintel. I would be concerned if you took away Linguintel's key employees for a competing venture.'

'Akshay, I really don't know why you're being so paranoid. GK was my first employee at Linguintel. Has he told you...'

'He'll tell me now.'

GK walked on to the terrace followed by the attendant and bouncer.

'Hello boss,' he said to me. He turned to Bhalla, 'Hello sir.'

'Hi Hejamady. Whiskey and water on ice?' Bhalla asked him.

'Sure sir.'

The valet made him a drink.

Hejamady looked at the bottle. 'What happened sir? You are also cost saving?'

'That was Harish's choice, Hejamady.' Bhalla sounded venomous. 'You know I wouldn't drink this stuff.'

GK reached for the humidor and pulled out a cigar. He turned to me. 'Got a light boss?'

Bhalla scowled. 'Here.' He clipped the end of the cigar and held up a cigar lighter.

'So, what are you two fuckers up to?' Bhalla spat out the words.

'Actually, Akshay, I should be asking you that. Why are you spying on me?'

'Sogacorp is a competitor. I'm interested in what they're up to, especially when it concerns my business.'

'It doesn't anymore. You gave me a full buyout. You didn't let me keep even one per cent of my equity. I have nothing to do with Linguintel since the buyout.'

'Then why is it—the afternoon that you return to Delhi you go out for drinks with Hejamady?'

'Because we have a history—he was my first employee—Linguintel was built on his back. Go back into the system and pull out the first sixteen thousand records...'

'Seventeen thousand four hundred eighty-six,' GK interrupted.

'Right—and see who entered or verified them.'

'I swear Harish—if you or Hejamady are trying to screw me.'

He turned to GK, 'Hejamady, your fucking buyout will go to zero really fucking fast.'

Hejamady's cigar stopped half-way to his mouth. 'Sir, can we speak privately?'

'You and me?' Bhalla barked.

'No, tell the waiter and bouncer to go away.'

Bhalla raised his hand and flicked his wrist. Both the men retreated indoors.

GK sat back in the chair and cackled. 'The buyout sir? That is not even a threat. You don't even know our history. I was a waiter in a bloody shit bar when Harish gave me the job. Your four-crore buyout is nothing. It's not going to change my life.'

'Hejamady, easy,' I said.

'No. That's why I told him to send the staff away.'

He turned to Bhalla. 'Do you really think money is everything? Do you think this house of yours makes me respect you? Do you think I am afraid of that bouncer? When I worked in the bar, I have bashed twenty—thirty guys like that—sometimes two and three at one time.'

'GK, Shut Up,' I said. 'Akshay—what exactly is your concern?'

'What are you doing hanging out with Soga?'

'Nothing. Just hanging out like you said. Partying a little.'

'You're partying with Soga?'

'Well, he doesn't really party by your definition, but I do have an entertaining time with his people.'

'OK, but no business?'

'A little business, but nothing that would be a threat to Linguintel.'

'What business?'

'I'm not going to tell you that Akshay. I don't owe you an answer on that.'

'Harish, I beat Soga to one deal. When there are some numbers on the table, let me know. I'll beat him again.'

'I'll think about that. Are we done?'

'No wait—one more drink,' GK said.

I wasn't scared of Bhalla anymore, but I didn't want

him as an enemy. 'GK, shut up. You're in the man's house—you have to show him respect.'

'Sorry boss.' He slapped his own head as if in atonement and retreated to the back of his chair.

I turned to Bhalla. 'Akshay, I apologise for his behaviour. You must know by now that he's a nutcase. The only reason I hired him is because none of my data entry operators stuck around for more than a week, and it turns out you had to be a certain kind of crazy to last those first five years.'

Bhalla's eyes shifted between GK and me—radiating fury.

'Now. You called me here for a reason. You're concerned about me hanging out with Soga and meeting with GK, and you're wondering if I'm trying to sabotage Linguintel in some way. I am not.'

'Go on,' he said—cooling down a bit.

'I met Hiroto Soga through mutual friends, and we have met socially a few times. Yes, we talk about business, and yes, he's unhappy about losing the Linguintel deal, but it's in the past for him and we are not looking to do anything that will harm your interests.'

'You better be fucking sure about that Harish,' Bhalla said. 'I will fuck up your life if you cross me in any way.'

'Akshay, I'm aware of the lengths you go to protect your image and prestige. I have enough problems of my own—with my divorce et cetera and I don't need any more. So please—let's just have another drink and let's call it a dramatic but eventually pleasant evening.'

Bhalla appeared to squeeze the corner of the table and sat back. The valet walked and made another round of drinks. A tense silence hung in the air that eased slowly as the three of us sat on that terrace sipping Hibiki on ice.

Chapter 10

Chandni Chowk is a different experience for a photographer.

Under normal circumstances, the hawkers, touts, and backpackers are an inconvenience, and the brash electric rickshaws are mildly alarming. Today, however, with one eye closed, camera covering my face, messenger bag slung across my body—I feel uncomfortably vulnerable. In this old-world market the action, dust, and crowding seem as if it can't get any denser—unless, as I discovered, you're looking through a 35 mm lens. It sharpened things. It fed my senses more. Though hampered by my anxiety and feeling of nakedness, I felt more aware.

The Nikomat's mirror clacked as I took a picture.

'*Arrey, idhar se le na*!' a hawker shouted. He pointed at the architectural details of a dilapidated building that once was, 'The Imperial Bank of India'. The hawker's advice was good. Standing right beside him, I got a really good shot of this Ozymandian relic in a dusty and crowded marketplace. The hawker took a picture with his cell phone and showed it to me on a cracked screen under a peeling screen protector. He did a pretty good job framing—perhaps better than I had done. He asked to see my picture and I had to explain that I was shooting film.

I looked for Chaaya and saw her about fifty feet ahead of me. I followed her into a narrow passageway that turned out to be a camera market. Tiny cramped shops displayed all sorts of camera ware—digital, film, lenses, what have you. We headed up a flight of narrow stairs and stopped at what looked like a plywood booth. Chaaya looked up at an unlit bulb over the door and knocked.

A sliding door opened and a short, gaunt man with a fuzzy grey head and coke-bottle glasses appeared. He smelt of sweat and vinegar—in fact, the booth smelt as if he had been marinating in there.

'Haan, bolo,' he said to me, sounding offended.

I shrugged and looked at Chaaya, who handed him a Ziploc of film rolls. He pushed his glasses up and held the bag three inches from his face. His face relaxed into a smile.

He raised his index finger. 'Madam from Baxterpuri?' He stepped closer and looked at her face from six inches away.

'Yes uncle. Dechen bhaiya has been sending my rolls.'

Then I noticed it—like the lenses and cameras, the Dwidala Camera lotus bud motif was on the film cassettes too.

'Come in, come in ma'am.'

The booth was divided into two sections—a seating space that was packed with plastic boxes and a chest freezer—and an inner section, separated by a sliding door that appeared to be a dark room.

Chaaya turned to me. 'This is Mr Dwarkanath. He has been processing my rolls ever since Bhikshu Dechen got me hooked on film.'

Dwarkanath gave us a tour of the space. Much of what he said—including the names of the enlargers, didn't register.

'Uncle, we have to go handle some other things,' Chaaya said. 'I'll call you in a few days and come to pick up the prints.'

Dwarkanath looked at his watch. 'Will be ready on Saturday morning madam. Confirm.'

'Very good! Thanks!'

'Wait.' The old man turned around to rummage in the chest freezer. In a few moments, he turned up with a small yellow and red box. Film obviously.

Chaaya examined it. 'Are you serious?'

The old man smiled.

'Who will process it Uncle? Kodak Bombay hasn't processed this since 1986!'

'Dwarkanath will process,' he said, and slid the plywood door shut.

In the shower that night, I reflected on this day of

contrasts. The dust, chaos, and anxiety of Old Delhi was now washing off my body, and I would soon towel myself dry and turn to the comfort, familiarity, and warmth of Chaaya's body. The mystery of that roll that Dwarkanath gave her—nagged me, and she would have explained had I asked—but I decided to let it reveal itself when it does.

'Tired?' Chaaya asked me.

'A little,' I muttered, sliding into bed.

'What's on your mind?'

'Plenty of things. The legal cases, what to do when Srishti is back in town, what Akshay Bhalla may be up to, what Hiroto wants with me…'

'Let me lighten the load,' she said softly. The legal cases, Darbari will sort them out. As to Hiroto, he's not a schemer—he will tell you what he wants when he feels the time is right. About Srishti coming to town, what do you want to do?'

'I want to see her.'

'Talk to Darbari about that one of these days. He'll tell you what to do.'

Darbari is magic. As soon as he had entered the picture the other day, both my lawyers shaped up. No more vague text messages, no more one-line emails, no more unanswered calls. I set a date for a meeting and both of them accepted without protest. His office was what you expect an old-world lawyer's to be. A wall of books—not just law, but literature and history too. Oak wainscotting, timber furniture, Persian carpets from wall to wall—and an Eames lounge chair by the window with a Nakamichi audio system beside it.

Both my lawyers showed up with thick files that I had never seen before. Darbari reclined on the Eames chair with his feet up on the footstool and the files in his lap. On a peg table beside him, lay a notepad and a fountain pen. He read through the files, marking pages and making notes on the pad. Ever so often, he would slow blink and look at one of the lawyers over his reading glasses. You could actually see them tremble when he did that.

We sat in silence for about three hours. When he was done, he ripped five sheets off the pad, stuck three of them in my divorce file, and two in my criminal file.

'Counsellors, let's reconvene next week. Please work on my notes and have these petitions ready as I recommended.'

'There is one more thing Mr Darbari,' I said. 'Sameera and Srishti are coming to India for a wedding next month. Is there a way I could see my daughter?'

'No,' he said. 'Your counsellors and I are building a delicate case to extricate you from this mess. Lawyering is a lot about perspective. I don't want you to do something that could be used against you. It will lead to more delays, more petitions, and more legal fees.'

'I haven't seen her for two years sir.'

'I empathise. I promise you this—in a few weeks, Sameera will bring your Srishti to meet you herself.'

I drove back home in a funk.

I told Chaaya about the meeting, and she was optimistic. 'Well, if Darbari says she'll bring Srishti to you, that is exactly how it will happen.'

'Seriously? Oh, come on. Sounds like some serious wishful thinking here.'

'Darling, you don't know KD. He's been a lawyer for 40 years—he's worked in human rights, international arbitrations, what have you. He's been a speaker at Davos even.'

'Sounds like hogwash to me. At least Seeta and Shankar had been up-front about the challenges in this case. Darbari? You know those fortune tellers who read a card that a parrot picks up? That's what he sounds like.'

Chaaya's cheeks reddened. 'Okay, shut up! Just shut the fuck up.'

I didn't expect that reaction. 'What? Seriously? Why would you talk to me like that?'

'KD is a very close friend. My family has known his family for nearly a century. He knows things about me that my own parents don't know. So, when you talk about him, you show some fucking respect.' She shoved me with both hands for emphasis.

Great. Our first couple fight.

I apologised first thing in the morning.

Something about being out with a camera just slows you down. No—your cell phone camera is not the same thing—not even the iPhone. Even the process of making a picture is different. With your cell phone, you see what you took, and you get to retake it, if you didn't get it right. It's different with film. The image that you took is stuck in a metal box—sensitive to light and heat, and can only be set free in pitch darkness by someone like Dwarkanath.

You're watching the world through a viewfinder—with my FTN, it covers 92 per cent of the image that you actually get on film. So, what you get is not exactly what you see. This slice of experience that Bhikshu Dechen likes to go on about is not exactly what you save on film. But well, that's the same for memory too, isn't it? Like what GK remembers of the night when we went out to celebrate the VC funding. So maybe the photograph is a little more than a slice of experience, but certainly more accurate than just a memory.

Then the slicing itself is capricious and excluding because the moment you press the shutter button, the camera's mirror slaps up blocking out the viewfinder, the shutter opens and exposes the film, and the slice you captured is actually the slice you missed. Oh hell. I'd found a hole in Bhikshu Dechen's thesis.

Lodhi Garden is a weird place to be taking pictures—lovers behind the bushes and trees; important men and women—cabinet ministers, diplomats, spies, and bureaucrats taking a stroll—this cohort are often accompanied by armed plainclothesmen, who are easily identified by their safari suit and sports shoes ensemble. Everyone seems wary of someone with a camera. Chaaya and I contented ourselves with taking pictures of turrets and the ruined courtyard beside Sikandar Lodhi's tomb. I wasn't feeling it.

We lunched in near silence at an expensive but mediocre restaurant that adjoined Lodi Garden.

I looked at her as we waited for our appetizers. She had begun to tan a bit, and a sheen of sweat covered her face.

'So, what's your story?' I asked her.

She seemed surprised. 'What do you mean?'

'Who is Chaaya Singh? How did she end up on a mountain in Uttarakhand?'

She laughed. 'Finally, the important questions. After sleeping with me for three months!'

'Short answer—typical Delhi girl. My parents are Civil Servants—father is in the IAS, mother in the Revenue Service. I went to college in the UK and worked at an investment bank for a few years. The Baxter Lodge opportunity came up and I jumped at it.'

'You gave up investment banking to work at a hotel?'

She spluttered into laughter. I knew I had screwed up. 'Darling, I quit investment banking and bought a hotel. I own Baxter Lodge with four other shareholders.'

'I'm sorry. I'm just—'

'Stupid,' she said. 'Stupid in a forgivable way I mean. That's always everyone's first impression.'

'Do your parents know about us?'

'I'm sure they have some sort of an idea.'

My pulse quickened. 'Do you think I'll meet them soon?'

Chaaya smiled at me. 'I like where this is going. No. You're not going to meet them soon. I can't tell my parents that I'm dating a married man. I hope you get Darbari on the job so that you can be respectably divorced and still have enough money left so that my parents wouldn't be too disappointed.'

'Wow. OK.'

'There's also that you're still stuck up on your ex.'

'We have a child,' I said.

'Yes, but I get the sense that you're stuck up on your ex.' She sat back. 'Sometimes men have trouble letting go if they're not the one who did the breaking up.'

'She just disappeared one morning, taking my daughter with her.'

'What did you do to bring her back?'

'A week later, the police arrested me for domestic violence and dowry harassment.'

'In that one week, what did you do to bring them back?'

I'm sure she understood by the silence that I had done nothing.

As we pulled up to my building that evening, Chaaya put her hand on my shoulder. 'Find out about the wedding schedule. I'll figure something out.'

We were chilling at home when GK called.

'Hello boss.'

'Hey GK, what's up?'

'Boss, what's this place where your GF works?'

'Baxter Lodge, guru. Why?'

'Let's all go together for a trip no, Gurgaon is getting bloody hot.'

He obviously had something from the database query.

'Friday morning?' I suggested.

'Sure boss. Just like Bangalore-Udupi in the old days.'

'Exactly. We'll take my car.'

Come Friday, GK, Chaaya and I packed into the Toyota and headed to Baxterpur. Yes—it was just like Bangalore-Udupi. Back when we were running Linguintel in Bangalore, GK and I drove down to Udupi—his hometown—a couple of times a year. We would blast Kannada movie music and drive two-hour shifts and he would chain smoke for what was a 12-hour drive in those days. While GK would spend time with his parents, I would check into a seaside inn and just chill out. It was a great way for me to relax with beer and seafood without being in the midst of the crowds, expense, and the hype of Goa.

GK had become a better driver. He didn't smoke in the car, though we did stop for smoke breaks when we changed driver duty. For the music, we deferred to Chaaya's colourful apple playlist.

We reached Baxterpur in the evening and had dinner at Baxter Lodge. GK and I returned to Hillcrest for the night.

I made drinks.

'So, what did you find?' I asked him.

GK reached into his backpack and pulled out a pale green A4 sized envelope. 'This is what you need.' He tossed it on to the coffee table between us.

My heart started thumping and goosebumps rose on my skin. My hands began to tremble. I sat down and sipped my whiskey.

'Is that it?' I asked him with a quiver in my voice.

'Yes.'

'Did you zero in on one specific person?'

'Yes.'

'No doubt?'

'It's a 89.2% match and the next one is 69.5%.'

I stared at the envelope for a minute. I felt a sense of anticipation—sensations on my skin, the tremor in my hands—an electric current running through my cheeks and ears—but inside, I felt nothing. Nothing on the inside. This quest of mine, was it even real? Puran's face flashed before me. I recalled his anxiousness on that last night when he told me about Linguistic Intelligence, before he went to his room and hung himself. Then it all came back to me. The rage, the sadness, the pointlessness of it all. I grabbed the envelope and ripped it open.

Jaydip Bhat. Electronics Engineering. Our batch. It would have been an easy guess actually—the class knave. Mean, scheming, physically too weak to be a bully, but full of snark and derision.

GK reached into his backpack again and pulled out a Lenovo ThinkPad.

'Boss, if you're going to be checking this guy online, use this Tails OS laptop. So that you don't leave any metadata around his profile.'

This guy fucking thinks of everything.

Jaydip had done alright. After finishing his engineering with us, he worked at an IT company in Pune for a couple of years and then attended a top tier business school. Pretty much the standard track for an engineer in the noughts. He was now in Bangalore, working as the Chief Operating Officer for an IT company.

I finished my drink and headed to my bedroom. I lay awake all night running scenarios through my head. Should I confront him? Should I put out a hit on him? How much would it cost to abduct him and kill him somewhere remote? No that's absurd. What about closure?

Is there any such thing as closure?

All the loose ends in my life emerged from the corners of the room and did a silent dance in the darkness above my bed—Srishti, Puran, Sameera, my father—whirled in the ether and taunted me in whispers. Everything that I left incomplete—paintings from kindergarten, competitive exams from school, startup ideas that I didn't follow through on—swam in the darkness. Nausea crept up on me. I ran to the toilet and threw up. I washed my face and returned to my bed.

Chapter 11

'Not everything needs to be finished.' Bhikshu Dechen said between slurps of soup. 'The more we reckon life as a competition—a list of things to do, experience, complete—the more we set ourselves up for sadness.

'But some things need to be completed.'

'Why?'

'Because life demands it. Your obligations—your duty—your promises.'

'Bonds. Bondage.'

'Well, yes.'

'Promises. This is one reason that monks take a vow of silence. Words create bondage without us even knowing it. But back to topic. Attention. That's the key. The world is a noisy place. When something needs to be done, you need the ability to focus—observe, and resolve.'

'Resolving things is not easy.'

'I don't know how long you spent with Lama Phuntsok,

but I'm sure he may have mentioned—if you just observe your problems, the solutions come to you—sometimes they solve themselves, and sometimes they create the circumstances for you to act.'

'Well, that's easy to say.'

'You know, the deepest illusion of Samsara is that you matter. That you matter, and that you need to do something—you don't. You're just a speck in an incomprehensible universe. You did not matter before you were born, and you do not matter after you die. You are loved, mourned, hated, admired—all because of the bondage of others—the bondage of others to the illusion of you.'

'There's this man. He wronged a friend of mine and got away with it. Someone's got to make him pay.'

'The karmic state of the universe is always in balance. It balances itself. You can't go and upset it; it is not to be played with.

'Then—what should I do? Just let it go?'

'I see turmoil in your eyes. It's not anger. It's disappointment. Is it with yourself?'

I turned back to my food. It's funny how talking at a meal takes away your sense of taste. The food at this place was always top notch.

The monk finished his meal and went to the storage cases. He pulled out a massive lens and put it on the counter. When I finished my meal, I walked up to it.

He announced, '300 mm F 4.5.'

'Sometimes you just need to step far, far away and observe.'

The monk thought that the 35mm lens for my Fuji camera was a fair trade for the Nikon 35 mm from the last time, the 300 mm, and 20 rolls of the Eastman 5222 film.

Observe.

Jaydip's office was located in a large mixed-use complex in Central Bangalore. Bars and coffee shops on the lower floors of the building gave a great view of most open spaces. I identified the tower that he worked in and positioned myself at a coffee shop with a view of the entrance. It was 8 am, and the coffee shop was busy with Americano and health shake orders from people in gym outfits. At 9 am, a number of early-career types dropped by for take-away sandwiches, while two older men sat down for an English breakfast in what appeared to be a weekly ritual.

The crowd thickened. People came into their offices. I got up from the coffee shop and moved to the bar that was across from the coffee shop. The morning coffee crowd rolled into the leisure crowd—young people on coffee dates or shopping trips, surprisingly high numbers for a weekday—then the MLM hustlers—sharing life-changing business plans. I stood up and walked around, surveying the area to see if there was another entry to the office towers. There was, but it lacked a place from where I could observe without drawing attention to myself. I returned to the bar and sat down at a table with a view of the tower entrance. I took out my laptop and cleared my mailbox, and then put on some music to listen through my headphones while I waited.

At about 3 pm, a man walked out of the office tower lift and entered the coffee shop. He waved to the Barista, who immediately got busy with his coffee machine. He made a card payment at the billing desk, and stood there chatting with the girl behind the cash register. Obviously a regular with a standard order. He turned to look across the courtyard, when I caught sight of his face. I was quite sure it was him. Of course he looked very little like his LinkedIn display picture, so I needed a way to make sure. He picked up his coffee and walked back to the lift without me getting another good look at his face.

The next day, I walked into the coffee shop at 2 pm. No Jaydip Bhat until 5 pm.

The day after, I had better luck. At 10 am, I was tucking into an English Breakfast when the man walked in with a black strolley.

'Hey Srini! Got my coffee?'

It was him. Unmistakable. Perhaps 10 kilos heavier than his college days—a fit weekend warrior face—well styled hair, with some grey showing through.

'Didn't see you yesterday sir,' said the lady at the cash register.

'Travelling. Was in Hong Kong for a meeting. Just got

back—straight here from the airport!'

Her next words were drowned out by the roar of the coffee grinder.

Jaydip laughed.

Pale brown chinos that showed wrinkles from being on a flight. A cream linen shirt. Black shoes—he had obviously been in a dark suit for his meeting in Hong Kong. Apple Smartwatch.

As he pulled his phone from his pocket, a Volvo fob tumbled out. He squatted effortlessly to pick it up. Fucking cross fitter.

I shifted to the bar for lunch, and at 3:18 Jaydip Bhat came down for his coffee.

I returned to the serviced apartment and looked through my deliveries. I had given GK a shopping list, and he had been scouring Delhi's Nehru Place market for the things I needed. I set up a soldering station and got to work. My engineering degree did not teach me a single fucking thing of value to Linguintel, but I learned to solder in electronics lab class. I actually liked the smell of the wax and solder. I found myself humming through the job, despite my intense focus on the fine tip under the magnifying glass. What if the police walked in right now? They'd think they found a bomb factory.

The next day, I went down to the basement parking area of Jaydip's office. The building's management had been kind enough to mark parking slots with company logos, and Jaydip's company had about a hundred spaces for cars. I found the only Volvo—a steel grey S90—parked between a white Toyota and a blue BMW.

I walked around for a bit—the only CCTV cameras in the parking area were for the entrances. I pulled out my thumb-sized GPS tracker that I had hacked to draw power from a 20,000 mAh power bank, and fixed it to the underside of his front bumper. The car had just been washed, so the 3M double sided tape that I used on both the tracker and battery pack made a fantastic bond. I returned to the bar and did a systems check. I wasn't seeing a signal—perhaps due to the car being in the basement. But the way this tracker was designed, it would send me a message with GPS coordinates every minute. With nothing much to do but wait, I ordered a beer.

That evening, at about 7 pm, I got my first ping from the tracker. The next morning, I boarded a flight to Delhi.

Darbari had called a meeting with my lawyers. This time though, he sat at his desk, looking through the files, marking the pages with his fountain pen. The lawyers and I sat across from him, watching the shadows from the setting sun lengthen on the table and eventually disappear into the soft lighting from the Tiffany's lamps in the room. He finished my divorce lawyer's file and turned to the criminal lawyer's papers. Halfway through, he stopped, dropped his shoulders with a sigh and scored two pages from corner to corner. He pulled out a sheet of paper from a folder on his desk and spent about fifteen minutes covering it in deliberate and measured handwriting. He didn't pause for even a second to think or correct anything. Just a steady left to right rhythm, dripping an elegant cursive on to the paper. Once done, he handed the files back and dismissed the lawyers.

I half-rose to ask his permission to leave, but he motioned with his finger, ordering me to sit. He leaned back in his swivel chair, and there was about sixty seconds of a heavy silence.

'I thought this would be a good time to talk about my fee,' he said.

'Sure. I was hoping to bring that up myself.'

He looked at his watch and then at me. 'Drink?' his fingers made that universal gesture that would be a small measure in a Collins glass and a large in an old-fashioned glass.

'Just a small one maybe,' I returned the gesture. 'I need to drive.'

He walked to the bar cabinet in the corner and put out two old fashioned whiskey glasses. 'How do you take your whiskey?'

'A little water, that's all.'

He poured out some Ballantine's in two glasses, added some water to mine, and came back to the table.

He took a sip and swallowed slowly. 'I wouldn't be too worried about this case. There's so much here that would be confounding to resolve, but between Delhi Police's exemplary investigative work and the Canadian Embassy's do-gooding, the only way that this will come through is in your favour. It's just a matter of time and restraint.'

'Restraint. What you called for the last time we spoke.'

'Are you serious about Chaaya?' His eyes were boring into mine.

Suddenly, I felt under intense pressure. Tendrils of ferocity seemed to emerge from somewhere deep within him and poke their way through his gentility. I half-expected his skin to crack from the corners of his eyes to his ears and from his forehead to his chin, and a snorting, red-eyed rhino to emerge.

'Yes,' I said. 'Look, it's been just a few weeks that we have known each other, but we get along very well, and I think we have similar feelings for each other.'

The tendrils of ferocity receded a bit, but he didn't even blink.

I took a sip of my whiskey. 'This is the reason that I need this sorted out at the earliest. I do think I have a future with her, and I want a future with her, but that cannot happen unless my divorce comes through and all these legal cases are sorted. Until I met her, I was happy letting Seeta and Shankar take their time with these things, but I just don't want to wait anymore.'

He took another sip of his whiskey without letting his glass interrupt his stare. He finally blinked. 'I'll send you an email with details of my fee. My first payment will be due the day after Sameera brings Srishti to meet you. You will make the second payment the day after your joint custody agreement is signed.'

'Thank you.'

He got up from the table and went across the room to the music system. He popped in a cassette, and soft strains of an Indian classical raag swept through the room. He sat down in the Eames chair. 'Sorry. I'm not young anymore, and this legal reading takes a physical toll on me.'

'That's alright. Nice music.'

'Glad you like it.'

He closed his eyes and put his heels up on the Eames footstool. 'Raag Yaman. Hindustani music classifies pieces by the time of day they should be listened to. It really works for me. Make yourself another drink if you like and see yourself out when you please.'

I sat there sipping my whiskey and listening to the music. Darbari was a study in vulnerability. This powerful, eminent, and successful lawyer—articulate, and intelligent—here in this room that represents his identity, erudition, achievements, and power. In this room, where mere minutes ago he bristled with annoyance at the work of my lawyers, and then burned with a silent intensity when he asked me about Chaaya, he now lay supine on a fancy chair, half asleep, jugular exposed, in the company of a man he had only known for a few days.

When the music slowed to a pause, I left.

Canada Dry again. Chaaya got a Gold Spot. I should ask her that story sometime, though I'm sure that it would be as mundane as mine.

'Ooof, I never tire of lunch here.' She took a hit of the Gold Spot before digging into her meal.

The monk smiled. 'I never tire of seeing you.'

'If it wasn't your Celibacy vow, I would say that you're hitting on me.'

The monk smiled. 'Well, detaching lust from human connections makes things so much simpler, and so much more fun.'

I rolled my eyes so hard that you could hear them grind.

'I need a new camera,' Chaaya said. 'Something… compact. Nice lens closer to normal than wide—so forty-ish. Oh, and it's for low light use, so it must be fast—f/2 or wider maximum aperture.'

The monk ate in silence for about a minute.

'Rough handling?' he finally asked.

'No.'

'I have something,' he said and carried on with his meal.

When we finished and were tucking through small helpings of that Tibetan cheesecake thing—I forget the ethnic word for it—the monk went up to his display case and pulled out a camera. Her mouth still full, Chaaya rose to her feet. The monk made the 'no' gesture with his index finger and pointed to her stool.

Chaaya complied. She patiently finished her dessert, scraping every last speck off the saucer and then got up.

'Olympus 35 LC,' the monk said, sliding the camera over the counter.

'Really now.'

'There's nothing better,' he tilted the lens up at her. 'Zuiko 42 mm lens. Its field of view is exactly equal to the central vision span of the human eye. Takes in exactly what you would look at with intention. It's a better lens than anything Leica made at the time.'

'It's a rangefinder,' Chaaya deadpanned.

'Yes. That makes it light, and small. The frameline window increases the brightness of the image in the viewfinder. Shoot Eastman 5222 at 1600 and ask Dwarkanath to process in a fine-grain developer.'

'Fine grain?'

'Yes,' the monk nodded. 'LED mood lighting. Looks bright, but no sharpness. Dwarkanath knows—just tell him it was LED lighting. Pushing to 1600 will add to the contrast.'

Chaaya's jaw dropped. She picked up the camera without another word.

We went back to Hillcrest cottage and smoked some Baxterpur Peach in the living room. I looked at my third phone that was tracking Jaydip Bhat's entire life. It's amazing how all our lives are just a repetition of a routine. Wake up, coffee, shit, shower, and shave, breakfast, commute, work, commute, dinner, sleep. Add alcohol for weekends, and maybe some sex if you're unmarried.

Each day, I downloaded the SMSes sent by the tracker to my laptop, pulled them into Google sheets, from where a python script would plot them on Google Maps. Jaydip's activities spanned a near-perfect rhombus on the map of Bangalore. Home, gym, work, and golf course. Another apartment perhaps twice a week. One weekend he drove to Coorg. Another time, he went on a two-day golf outing to Mysore. I learned so much about him with that cheap, fifty-dollar tracker and thirty-dollar battery pack. I flew to Bangalore.

Did something need to be done? I don't know. What did I want to do about Jaydip? I don't know. If it were college days again, perhaps I would have taken some sort of a stupid decision that I would have paid for my entire life. Six months ago? Perhaps a stupid decision that would have cost me a lot of money and anxiety. Today? With so much to lose—this wonderful woman I seem to be falling in love with, on the cusp of being able to rebuild with my child?

Was Lama Phuntsok, right? Was Bhikshu Dechen?

Tracking Jaydip was really easy. I had all his usual visits on the laptop. I would hang around at one of the bars or coffee shops in the lobby of his office and get ready when his car started moving. It was easy to guess where he would be going, and he was a pretty sedate driver—rarely exceeding 20 km/h. On second thought, that is actually the fastest you can drive in that shithole of a city.

The Nikkor Auto P 300 mm lens is really something. It's fucking huge—bigger than anything that you would commonly find on a consumer camera today. Put it on a Nikomat, and it really draws attention. Security guards will stop you to tell you that there's no photography allowed while people around them will be taking cell phone photographs. Smell powerful. Use Old Spice or something similarly musky-woody. Look important. Pleated trousers, dress shirt, pen in the breast-pocket, mechanical watch, leather shoes. Ask to see the sign that says 'No Photography Allowed'. If you really want to push it, wear a pale brown safari suit and brown shoes. Nobody will even look you in the eye.

The best part is that from the corner table at the bar, I was able to get a clear shot of Jaydip buying his coffee. Click. Hell, when the prints came back from Dwarkanath, I could read the branding on the cup.

That was him—corporate leader, the kind but tough type. The coffee shop staff liked him. Real smiles, a memory of his regular order, small talk. People recognised him. Nodded to him in the lobby. Click.

The golf club was a different matter. One of the few luxuries that I had splurged on when Linguintel was bought out, was a membership in one of the nicer clubs in Bhopal that gave you affiliate access to the nicer clubs in

Delhi that had a 50-year waiting list, and the nicest clubs in Bangalore that had a 100-year wait list. The Karnataka Golf Association doesn't even have a waiting list.

Smell powerful, look important. Lacoste shirt and white pants at the golf course. TaylorMade club set. Yes, this whole shadowing thing was getting really expensive.

'What pictures are you taking if I may ask?'

'The birds. You have some pond herons on the water hazard.'

'May I see?'

'Oh, I would love to show you. Let me send you the prints when I get the rolls developed.'

'Oh, you shoot film?'

Click.

'Yes. My golf partners are habitually late. I get a lot of good pictures while waiting for them.'

'Oh nice.'

Click.

A family man. A five-year-old and a toddler who like to swim on Sunday mornings. Pretty wife. Click. They like to go to Burger King where the toddler sucks French fries and sips ketchup, while Jaydip does his cheat meal of two double patty burgers and a large coke. These cross fitters, I tell you.

Click.

Then you realise, nobody really cares. Yes, you're walking around with this camera and a huge lens. You smell expensive and you look powerful. It actually draws much less attention than you expect.

'Sir, no photos allowed.'

'I'm not taking photos.'

'No photography sir.'

'My hands are in my pockets. I'm not taking any photographs.'

'Not allowed sir.'

'Why is that girl allowed to take a selfie, that guy allowed to take a picture of his food, but I'm not allowed to walk here with a camera?'

'Rules sir.'

'Show me the rule book.'

'I don't have.'

Fuck off, you think to yourself, and walk right on. Just think it, don't say it. Don't troll. Don't be memorable, don't make a scene.

Oh, is that a film camera? My uncle had one just like that.

Oh, a film camera? I didn't know you could get film these days.

Oh wow! Look, that guy has a film camera. Uncle, may I ask you a question? Why do you shoot film these days? Why not just use an iPhone? (Does your iPhone have a 300 mm lens?)

Oh, the Auto P. Lousy lens. Why would you use the Auto P? It's the most horrible Nikon lens I ever used. I used to go wildlife photographing with TNA Perumal in the 70s. I used one in Kabini in 1972 and all my pictures came out blurry. (Must have been your delirium tremens. Next!)

Oh wow, hey I'm analogue too—I listen to Vinyl's. (No words, fake smile, thumbs up.)

The other apartment was a mystery. The residents were obviously wealthy—the building had mostly German cars and a couple of superbikes in the outdoor parking slots. What would Jaydip be doing here on weekday afternoons? The data showed that he usually visited on Tuesday and Thursday before lunch, stayed a few hours, and then left. I saw that myself for two weeks running, and got pictures of him on two occasions.

The fifth time I trailed him there, it was different.

Just as I arrived, I saw him leave with someone else in the car. He was moving too fast for me to discern who it was. Not a problem. The tracker led me to a luxury hotel—1.15 pm—lunch obviously. Herein lay the problem—a coffee shop and three restaurants.

So, it's a Thursday afternoon—would Jaydip Bhat go for Indian, Italian, Fusion Asian, or just a cup of coffee? Coffee is out. There are nice coffee shops everywhere in Bangalore—he wouldn't drive ten kilometres for lobby coffee. Italian is out. There's refined grain in everything that will fuck up the keto paleo whatever that gives a 40-year-old man the jawline of a teenage athlete. Indian and fusion. I would say fusion—they have salads and stuff.

Obviously, I left the camera in the car.

Fusion it was. They had taken a table away from the door. I found a corner booth from where I had a view of their table. I couldn't hear their words.

A woman. She had obviously been waiting for him when he arrived at the apartment complex. She wore makeup, her hair had been done, she was prettier than his wife, younger too, mid 20s perhaps. She sat at the table, supporting her chin in her palm, elbow on the table, eyes dreamily gazing at him, faint smile on her lips. Very much in love. She did most of the talking—it seemed like a regular date.

She got a glass of white wine that she held the right way—Jaydip drank just water. I ordered a chimichurri steak with a side of couscous salad.

Their food arrived in about twenty minutes and mine shortly afterwards. They ate, with the woman still doing most of the talking—unintelligible scraps of Jaydip's voice blowing in my direction; he could make her laugh. Every time he said something, she would laugh. She was getting drunk by her third glass of wine, and it showed when she laughed.

They didn't have dessert.

I stayed at the restaurant and ordered my third beer.

Jaydeep drove back to her apartment—he didn't just drop her off—I could tell from the tracker data. He was fucking her. She was drunk, happy, and was now being fucked silly. Did she know that he was married? She must know. That's why they always meet on weekdays. Then, what kept her coming back? Had he promised to leave his wife and marry her?

Why do some men fuck things up so badly? He had a wife, two kids—his wife was attractive—less attractive than this woman, but not by much. Were she to wear makeup and dress for a date, perhaps prettier—my subjective view. When this thing hits the roof, he'll be the only winner. There will be two broken women—one heartbroken, one guilt stricken, two hurting children who would blame themselves for their father abandoning them.

Two hours. He stayed there fucking her for two hours, and then started moving again.

By then I'd had four beers. I checked into the hotel, slept it off and drove back to my serviced apartment the next morning.

Chaaya called when I was having breakfast. She wanted me back in Gurgaon. I changed the battery pack on the tracker that afternoon. I took the evening flight to Delhi and was home in time for dinner.

We'd adopted Hiroto's style of eating—cooking simple stuff while talking. She didn't know that I'd been stalking Puran's killer. She would have been angry. She never really asked what I had been up to. There was this quiet tension that had been building up between us. I think it had something to do with Sameera being back in town.

Suhani Gulati's wedding was just two days away.

'So, what have you been up to in Bangalore?' she asked between sips of Shiraz.

'Nothing much...just travelling, meeting up with some old college mates. Catching up on a lot of what I missed during the Linguintel days.'

'Did anything fun?'

'Not really. Just a lot of coffee shops, bars, and the golf course.'

'You went and bought a fucking TaylorMade golf set to just hang out at a golf course?'

'Well, it's part of the uniform, isn't it?'

Chaaya laughed. 'Not really. I think only a third of the members of the Delhi Golf Club own any gear. They just go there to drink and network. Only guests play any golf at all.'

'What have you been up to?' I asked her.

'Well, nothing much—clothes shopping for the wedding.'

'Wedding? I didn't know you were going to one.'

She took a thoughtful sip. 'I'm going to Suhani's wedding.'

'What?'

'Well, it's at the Imperial Hotel so the food should be good. Also, I'll probably get to see your wife.'

We moved our lamb gravy, garlic fried rice, and green leafy vinaigrette salad to the dining table.

'What made you decide to go to the wedding?'

'You can't go. I thought I'll go in there and get a picture of Srishti.'

The penny dropped. 'With the Olympus camera that Bhikshu Dechen gave you.'

'Yeah.'

'Isn't is risky?'

'Not at all. Your wife doesn't know me, any guests who know me wouldn't be surprised to see me there. Tch! It's Delhi. All us Civil Service brats are related.'

'Knowing that family, I'm sure there are going to be some really important people there. Definitely someone from the Home Ministry, at least one Supreme Court Judge, a couple of generals, at least two dozen IAS officers. The place will be crawling with armed guards.'

She pinched my nose. 'Don't worry! Nobody is going to shoot a girl wearing Sabyasachi for dropping by a wedding uninvited. It would totally fuck up the embroidery.' She snorted at her own joke. 'Besides, with all the big shots who will be attending, they won't even be checking invitations. There will be five-six hundred guests for sure.'

A beige *lehnga* and a cream blouse, with delicate and minimal filigree work, paired with a gold georgette dupatta. Chaaya really knows how to dress up. Whether the quiet elegance in her job at the Baxter Lodge—her pragmatic stylishness while rambling around the hills taking photographs—or today—dressed in the silks and sequins of a wedding guest.

I sat and watched her as she put on her makeup.

'I want to take a picture,' I said.

'Oooh! Let's do one Maharani style.'

She draped the dupatta over her head and shoulders while I picked up the Nikomat and 35 mm lens. I positioned her at the dining table with its faux Queen Anne chairs and Victorian style candlestick. She looked longingly into the soft evening light that came through the window—yes, she did look like a princess.

Click.

She then turned to me and brought the dupatta down as a veil. The dupatta shimmered in the setting sun—its embellishments twinkling—and the room visibly inched towards darkness.

Click.

The light faded out.

I walked her down to the car—a steel grey Mercedes probably from the 1980s.

'Borrowed it from Darbari.' She winked.

A grey-haired chauffeur in a white uniform held the door open. He waited stoically as she gathered her skirt and settled in the back seat, and then shut the door with just the right amount of force. The car pulled away gently and floated into the chaos of Gurgaon's traffic.

I returned to the apartment.

Have you ever been terrified of losing someone to your past?

Something I said made her do this. Maybe that comment about not being able to see Srishti soon enough, maybe a comment that I let slip about not having a picture of what she looks like today. Maybe it was self-motivated—Chaaya wanting to see who this woman is, get a feel for what the other side of this story was.

Sameera never came for a single hearing of either the criminal case or the divorce case. Even her lawyer claimed that he had no idea of her whereabouts. She went on with her life in Canada, taking Srishti along, without even looking back. What is the other side of the story? I can't say. It would be good to know.

I moped around the apartment, my mind wandering to all the hurtful, scary, and shameful places in my life. Should have, would have, could have…If only.

I showered and went to bed at 10.30, but sleep eluded me.

Close to midnight, I heard Chaaya enter the apartment. I heard her change, as Guerlain Shalimar drifted across the bedroom, and she got into bed beside me.

'I didn't get shot,' she whispered. 'Your daughter is wonderful; she's such a joy. I'll leave the roll with Dwarkanath tomorrow morning.'

The next morning, she left before I woke up.

Emptiness—emptiness with a tinge of finality. Since we got together, there was always a sense of dread—when I woke up to an empty house. Bondage, the monk would call it. The agonies of bondage. Was it even realistic to just let go—the way the books and lectures say—to let things be—like the mushy quotes about love and relationships quoted, instagrammed, retweeted by the chronically broken hearted?

I phoned her, and we decided to meet at Lodhi garden. I took my Nikomat with the 35 mm lens.

Nothing had changed. She looked just as she did the previous afternoon. It seemed that we had survived her brush with my past. The light was good. I got a picture of her seated on the grass, smiling in the sun, with the Bada Gumbad behind her. A typical Lodhi Garden portrait that you would see on Instagram ten thousand times. In my head I could see how that would turn out. The Nikkor S 35 mm dates to the 1960s. At its widest aperture of F2.8 it helps freeze a subject in sharp detail, while gently blurring the background. You would still be able to tell that Chaaya was at Bada Gumbad. Given the direction of the sun, there would be a slight flare from the sun falling on the lens, but hey, it wouldn't be as bad as the glare from the sun falling in your eyes. This is where we were—I will have a print to remind me of this.

'So, what happened at the wedding?'

'Nothing much. I got in without any problems. Only seven children were around four years old—two girls among them. Sameera was chatting with Rishika and Vedika Gulati—Suhani's cousins. Srishti was in a little dark blue *lehenga* with a gold *choli*. If cuteness had a name, it would be her. I got two pictures. She danced at one of the cousin dances—even got most of the steps right!

A knot formed in my throat. I could feel tears build up. My body felt of emptiness. A deep dark emptiness—no thoughts, no feelings, just this empty sadness—from which there seemed to be no escape. Sitting in the sun there at Lodhi garden, I felt cold.

'Hey,' Chaaya said softly. 'Seriously, it's just a matter of a few weeks. Darbari is on the case.'

Two days later, we went to meet Dwarkanath. He had made postcard sized prints. I saw Srishti for the first time in two years. Her baby face was now a little girl's face—she was smiling—radiating joy. She had long, curly hair that seemed to have been professionally styled for the wedding. My child.

My eyes filled with tears and my knees buckled. I sat with a thud on the floor of Dwarkanath's shop. He sat down beside me and put his hand on my knee.

'Your daughter?'

'Yes. Can you make a wallet sized print?'

'Yes, and I'll laminate it. It will last hundred years.'

Chaaya drove us back.

Darbari called me. We had a court hearing the week after.

Chapter 12

My memories of the Delhi District Courts are traumatic. The first time, I had been taken from a foul-smelling holding area in Tihar Jail in a foul-smelling bus to the court building—handcuffed. My bus mates were a rapist; seven members of a criminal gang that murdered a businessman; a mentally unstable murderer; and about a dozen others I didn't really hear about in the undertrial ward. I was before the judge for just 30 seconds before she extended my remand for a month. I stayed in jail for nearly four months—mainly because the papers had carried the story of the Linguintel buyout, and my lawyer had received several 'bail for cash' offers that he had refused. The gang members, and most of the other under-trails got bail way before me. The gang members offered to 'fix' the situation for a fee. I declined obviously.

This time, the judge called the case, and perhaps it was Darbari's stature as a lawyer or the figure he cut in court—black jacket, crisp advocate's collar, striped trousers, legal gown—that he heard him out. Darbari spoke for about fifteen minutes, recounting the facts of the case, the reason why Atwal summoned me to the police station from Baxterpur, and how this ongoing legal matter was impacting my ability to earn a livelihood.

The judge called for Atwal, but he wasn't present in court. She asked for a summons to be sent to him to attend court the next Monday.

The next Monday, Atwal did not show up. Neither did he respond to the summons. The judge quashed the FIR and accepted an application for the return of my passport.

We drove back from the court in near silence.

'Well, that's one down,' Chaaya said.

'Yup. Things are changing.'

And change they did.

The next week, Hiroto returned to Baxterpur.

The Boadicea lily tea was now familiar.

I floated into the dark goldness pulsing, trembling, body feeling on fire, but cold at the same time—not painfully so, it's inexplicable in words in any case.

Bunky the Purple Monkey floated into view, and this time, Bhikshu Dechen was seated cross-legged between his ears.

'Oh anxiety. So much anxiety,' the monk said.

I didn't say anything.

'Oh anxiety, so much anxiety,' Bunky said in

a little child's voice.

The monk caressed Bunky's fur.

'All your torment is self-inflicted,' Bunky said. 'Don't I know what you're thinking? Lying there in the darkness your thoughts scream to me. They scream to me and I can't sleep. I see you in Chaaya's arms—a place where any man would be so happy. Do you know that we dance when you're not at home? We put on boogie woogie videos on YouTube and she holds me, and we dance. I'm happy in her arms. Why aren't you? She told me that Srishti is coming back soon. I'm so happy. Why aren't you?'

'Bondage,' the monk said.

'Explain yourself fatso. Haha! He doesn't understand your Zen bullshit.' It sounded funny only because it was a little child's voice.

'You know Bunky, my purple monkey,' the monk said lovingly, without the slightest hint of sarcasm, 'this world is a prison, a prison where people do not know the difference between fun and bliss. People do things to their minds, and bodies that are fun, but fun is a very poor substitute for bliss. You keep seeking fun, and you need to keep taking it like a drug. People don't know bliss.'

'Especially not this fuckface,' Bunky interjected. 'Booze is not bliss. Neither is… Wooo-hooo. No, I won't say it, I won't say it. I don't want to hurt your feelings fatso. Keep talking.'

'People are bonded to their suffering,' the monk

continued. 'They don't understand that everything that they desire, everything that they possess, hurts them. It hurts others. But him, it's anxiety.' The monk looked me in the eye. 'Your mind. One small thing, and it's off! Just take one thought and you build a story out of it—a story that takes you deeper and deeper into suffering.'

'Deeper and deeper into suffering,' Bunky's voice echoed.

He said it over and over again, the echoes merged into an unintelligible, unbearably loud noise. I was on an escalator into a pit of fire. The escalator was descending; I was trying to climb away. Bunky and the monk were nowhere in sight. Acrid foul-smelling smoke came up from the pit. I kept trying to climb away but no matter how hard I tried, I just kept getting lower. I couldn't jump off—the escalator was over a bottomless darkness. I couldn't get away. I felt my legs and back get warm. Warmer. Hot. hotter. My clothes began to catch fire. I rolled over the side of the escalator into the nothingness. The dark goldness.

Bunky and the monk floated back into view.

'That was easy, wasn't it?' they said in unison.

'But he only did it when his arse was on fire literally,' Bunky said. 'Why do you have to wait until your arse is on fire?' Bunky laughed. 'Oh, and you're right. Bunky and the monk is a GRRREAT name for a Hip Hop band. Hey fatso, can you chant? I can rap, and you can chant the chorus. Haha!'

The dark goldness became thicker. I felt as if I was floating in an invisible goo. But wait, that's how I feel in life—as if everything that I do—getting up in the morning, brushing my teeth, taking a shit, driving, eating, drinking is against an invisible resistance. Is that what anxiety feels like?

'How do you live your entire life like this?' Bunky and the monk asked in unison.

The resistance to everything good. When you're pushed into doing the easier, not the important.

The resistance released, and in an instant, I was back to floating.

'Can we talk about his self-loathing?' the monk asked.

'Hahaha!' Bunky laughed, and then added in a man's voice—my voice, 'you hate yourself. Everything that you do, stems from the hate that you have for yourself. All the cruel things that you think about the people around you, you're actually channelling the hate that you have for yourself.'

'Then what should I do?' I asked.

'Accept yourself,' the monk said. 'Accept yourself and see the world as it is. Don't feel pressured to act—just let things unfold. Just let them unfold.'

'Accept yourself and let things unfold,' Bunky and the monk said.

'Enough with this stupid Zen bullshit,' I shouted. 'I've been going in circles with this nonsense for over a year now. First with Lama Phuntsok, and now with you.'

'I told you fatso, he doesn't understand your Zen bullshit.'

I began to spin in the nothingness. Faster and faster, I got really dizzy. I began to throw up—perhaps for a good fifteen minutes—my puke flying away into the darkness until I was just retching violently, with nothing left to expel.

The darkness eased into a sky-blue nothingness. I was on my back floating above a green sea under a clear blue sky.

'Can you imagine your life always being like this?' came the monk's voice. 'Just floating, just observing. Just letting the world unfold without thinking, judging, thinking how you want to react, what you want to say. There is so much for you to just observe.'

I spun down gently into a valley full of lilies. The valley full of lilies where Chaaya took me on our first date. I floated gently through the beautiful flowers, in the lush green valley, taking in the sights and sounds, the flowers, the bees, the ants. The last time I was here I was distracted by desire. Literally by how much I wanted to sleep with Chaaya.

'This guy is a lost fucking case,' came Bunky's voice. 'Horny, self-loathing, self-judging loser.'

No, I'm not. Let me back. Quiet. Quiet the mind.

Quiet this voice that follows me.

Gurgaon, Agra. Jaipur, Udaipur, Goa, Kollam, Kovalam, Munnar, Wayanad, Cochin, Comorin,

Pondicherry, Madras, Suryalanka, Anantpur, Hyderabad, Bidar, Hampi, Aurangabad, Bangalore, Mysore, Mangalore, Udupi, Murdeshwar, Bombay, Vapi, Kandla, Ahmedabad, Shimla, Manali, Pushkar, Baxterpur. Just running—running from this voice. Maybe I figured it out somewhere at the end, and that's why I signed up for Lama Phuntsok's meditation class. I knew that I had to quiet that voice. But the voice was threatened. Maybe it was working there for a while, but then it came back to me when I was in his class. The self-loathing that I began to direct at Phuntsok. If perhaps I had just stayed present, just listened…

'Aaaaaannd there he goes again…' came Bunky's voice. 'This…'

'Shhhh.' The monk cut him off. 'He's getting there.'

'OK. Shhh,' Bunky said in my voice.

There is that pushback from everything that is inside you. I remember Lama Phuntsok telling us about a world that thrives on anxiety. Ambition, commerce, social media, everything is structured on anxiety—fuelling or capitalising on a sense that you aren't enough, will not be enough, or are incomplete and need to be made whole. And this anxiety pulls one away from the people who only see the best in you—the ones who will always see you as whole, complete, and enough.

I floated through the lilies and up the crevice that led to the Boadicea lily. Sentinel lilies glowed with bright yellow centres and their luminous petals, lighting up the mouth of the cave. Inside, instead of the lilies, was Srishti—seated on a bed of glowing leaves, playing with Bunky the Purple Monkey. She looked up at me and smiled. Her eyes twinkled and she reached out to me. I reached for her and our fingers touched, but then, I began to float away. She smiled at me and waved. I wasn't ready to go. I tried to swim forwards but that's not the way this works of course. I heard faint voices—Adachi and Hiroto speaking in Japanese. Their voices faded out as I floated back up into the blue.

The ones who will always see you as whole, complete, and enough. My parents—my father—the lifelong municipal employee who spent his entire life providing and protecting. My mother—who kept our lives together in her own way. My grandmothers, always full of love and stories. Hejamady—who put up with my bad behaviour for 12 years. They swirled before me, smiling.

I was drawn upwards into the blue—then into the dark goldness—then slowly into the light. A ceiling fan appeared. I smelt Guerlain Shalimar. I was on a soft bed with Chaaya holding me, her cheek pressed into mine. She saw me stir and smiled at me.

There was a sharper—pungent smell. Puke. I got off the bed.

'Are you okay?' Chaaya asked.

I was wet with sweat. The front of my shirt had puke

stains. 'I don't know. What happened?'

'Nothing,' she said. 'Looks as if you had a really intense trip. You've been tripping for about 3 hours.'

We were in one of the bedrooms of Hiroto's suite. I stepped into the living room. Hiroto, Bushida and Adachi were in there, shirt sleeves rolled up, scrubbing down the couch and carpet. A Baxter Lodge bathrobe was on the floor with a pile of about twenty crumpled hand towels on it.

Hiroto looked at me and smiled. 'You look alright. Must have been an intense trip.'

'I don't know. Did I do all of this?' I asked, glancing at the towels.

'Don't worry about it,' Adachi said. He smiled. 'Take a shower.'

I went back into the room where I woke up. There they were again—white Lacoste T-Shirt and M&S Jeans.

I showered, changed, and went back into the living room.

This time, the Baxter Lodge housekeeping staff were in there, moving out the couch and carpets. They brought in a beige couch and a new carpet, and left.

We gathered around the kitchen counter. Bushida was beating some tempura batter. Hiroto poured me a glass of sake.

The first sip I took made me gag. It was the same sake—Sudo Honke that we had been drinking all this time, but the taste—this time the taste of the alcohol came right through. Hiroto peered at me and then looked at Chaaya. They smiled at each other. I tried another sip. It didn't work.

'I'm sorry—the sake is not working for me today,' I said.

'Not a problem,' Chaaya said, putting her hand on my wrist. She picked up the glass and emptied it in one gulp. 'Lemon soda? It will help you rehydrate.'

'Yes please.'

Chaaya walked up to the refrigerator and assembled the drink while Bushida and Hiroto got to work frying a batch of tempura. I basked in the lightness that I experienced every time after coming down from the Boadicea trip.

'So, what exactly is it with this lily?'

Hiroto took a sip of his sake and looked at me thoughtfully. 'Ok. Long story.'

'Let me hear it.'

'My family has assembled the world's largest collection of information on lilies over the past five hundred or so years. This repository has information on seventeen varieties across the world that are psychoactive and have accounts of use in mystical practices. The method of usage is similar—they're prepared in a tea with an alkaloid and fat base, and consumed. People speak of them as an awakening of sorts. You're just starting your process—I don't want to set any expectations.'

'I've never been keen on drugs,' I said.

'Well, this is an intoxicant, and yes, you may have taken it out of curiosity the first time, but you've taken it for the second and third times of your own volition. It must have added some value.'

'Well yes. A powerful experience.'

'I must warn you,' Hiroto said. 'These trips as a spiritual practice were used in very specific situations—in communities or groups that had built processes and rituals around them. If you've had some sort of an awakening for instance—you had a guide, a teacher, or a community—like a Sangha to help you navigate the process. This Boadicea lily for instance was used in Tibet by a Sangha of 13 Lamas. A space opened up only when one of them died. Now, those still alive are in Chinese detention. A similar lily in South America is used by Flower Shamans who guide you through a process of reflection in complete isolation. You live in the Shaman's hut. He feeds you from what he can forage in the forest. Every week, he asks you one question. No other communication takes place between the two of you, and you can talk to no other person for a year. Not a word. All you hear that one question and think about it for a week. All this time, you're on a complete plant diet—wild grains, fruits, leaves—no animal flesh and no intoxicants. At the end of fifty-one weeks, he gives you a potion and you trip for a whole week. I've met only one person who has completed this process.'

'What did he gain from it?'

'I didn't understand. It sounded like gibberish to me, but I'd like to believe that it was something so profound, that I just failed to understand it. Indeed, were I to tell you what I've gained by tripping on these lilies, you probably wouldn't understand. Unfortunately, most of these practices only survive in oral tradition for now. I've been able to build the process and ritual. We're working on the Sangha.'

It was my turn to fry tempura.

After dinner, Chaaya left and Hiroto asked me to stay for a while.

'So, do you feel up to talking about something serious?' he asked me.

'Sure.'

'Do you remember what we discussed about Linguintel?'

'Yes, I do. That was an interesting conversation.'

'If I buy it for you, could you make that happen?'

'I'll need to think about it. At the outset, it seems that my goals for Linguintel were really simplistic—obviously, it had a very narrow ambition in mind. Since I've left, they've done some pretty serious stuff—expanded the scope of what they can offer in terms of services, while training the system at the same time. Right now, I think this has potential far beyond even what you have in mind.'

'Can you make it happen?'

'I'm not sure. I've been completely out of the scene

for two years now. I have not kept up with technology, the industry, other M&As—with how fast this industry works, I would be starting from scratch.'

'I appreciate your honesty. I really do. Think about it for a couple of weeks, and let's meet in Delhi to discuss this again.'

'Alright.'

I returned to Hillcrest for the night.

Lama Phuntsok smiled at me as I took my seat at the edge of his class. In the first few minutes I began to regress—many of the negative thoughts that I had on my last day there seemed to return. I forced these from my mind. It was difficult to concentrate. My body hurt from sitting cross-legged on the floor. But the more I focused, I was able to squeeze some meaning from what he was saying.

We settled in for the meditation session. A disciple placed lit incense in the corners of the room. My internal dialogue started. I forced it out. Literally gritting my teeth.

A warm hand gently held my chin. I opened my eyes, and Lama Phuntsok was seated before me. I looked into his kind face and gentle eyes, taking in every crack, wrinkle, and mole.

'Relax your body,' he said to me. 'Tensing your body will bring anxiety, not clarity. Let the thoughts pass, don't react to them. Just let them pass through like water would pass through a sieve.'

I closed my eyes and relaxed my jaw. The thoughts

flowed, slowed down, and disappeared.

I entered the dark goldness. A tiny spot appeared in the distance; it grew bigger. Bunky. The monk was sitting cross-legged between his ears—meditating himself. Bunky grew bigger and floated right into me. His navel was a little knot of twine. The knot grew bigger as Bunky expanded. The twine looked as big as a rope. The shadows in it were the dark goldness, and I passed into them. It started again. My mind stayed clear as I passed infinitely through Bunky's navel.

I don't know how long I sat there. At one point, my body felt heavy. My legs turned to stone and my neck was stiff. I opened my eyes. The other meditators were gone. There were six monks sleeping on the floor around me. Lama Phuntsok was in front of me in lotus pose. He got up, helped me lie on the floor, and covered me with a coarse sheep wool blanket.

'Sleep.' He placed his palm on my forehead for a second and left.

I woke at dawn. The monks were already awake and meditating. I got up as quietly as I could, folded my blanket and left.

Seeing Baxterpur through the 35 mm lens was quite something. There was that clarity in seeing a little more than what appears to the eye. On the 15-minute walk from Hillcrest to Baxterpur market, I took just two photographs. Noon is not really a time for landscape photography.

'Nice to smell that you've gone back to Lama Phuntsok!' the monk said as soon as I walked into the shop.

'Smell?'

'The incense. The novitiates collect herbs from the mountains and make it at the monastery itself. You can't buy it anywhere. It's a rare smell—no camphor or sandalwood like you find in Indian incense.'

'Yes, it's been nice.'

'You're being polite. How do you feel?' He knocked on the shutter and the boy walked in with two cups of yak butter tea.

I took a sip of the tea and felt its warmth drip into my chest and sweep through my body. 'Really, I feel okay. Well, there is a sense of acceptance, but there's also a sense of foreboding. I realise that nothing in the world outside of this is designed to support the clarity that I experience in brief moments. In fact, everything seems designed to fight it and foil me. I'm beginning to understand the purpose of a Sangha.'

'You need to assemble it.'

'I know. It's frightening. You have no idea how many things are going on in my life right now.'

'Ah well, that's where a monk really can't relate. This has been my life from the time I was a child. I can't really put myself in the place of a man who has to deal with this world every day.'

'I have no idea how any of this is going to turn out.'

'There is nothing to be gained from knowing the future.'

'Well, perhaps there is.'

'Every spiritual practice has a different model of the future. Is it predestined? Then what is the point of knowing—but to fuel your anxiety? Can you act to change it? If so, given the complex workings of this world, how will you control everything to get what you want? It will be like herding monkeys. More anxiety. The best would be to be present, and let it play out. Ask Lama Phuntsok—he can explain it better than me.'

I stood there thoughtfully sipping my tea.

The monk sighed. He opened one of the little red boxes and pulled out a camera. 'Canon P. The lens is the 50mm f/0.95. The aperture of this lens is larger than its focal length. When they made this lens in the 1960s, they had to bend the laws of physics. It seems they bent the universe around it a little bit.'

The camera was beautiful. Similar to my Nikomat to hold, but with a more refined feel.

'How much is this worth?'

'Haha! The question now is—how much is it worth to you?'

I thought for a second and handed over my entire camera bag.

Bhikshu Dechen smiled. He opened the bag and lined up all my gear on the counter. My Fujifilm body, six

Fujifilm lenses, four batteries, and a charger; the Nikomat body, the 50mm f/2, and the 35 mm; and the Helios 44.

He set the Nikomat and the two Nikon lenses aside. 'These you will keep.' He waved his hand over the lined-up gear. 'All of this for that camera?'

'Yes.'

'You do realise that the material value of what you are giving me is probably higher than what you are getting in return?'

'Yes.'

The monk smiled. 'Come back anytime if you change your mind.'

He opened one of the other red boxes and pulled out a leather case and strap for the Canon. He ducked under the counter and brought out a brown leather bag identical to Doctor Bhatnagar's valise. The inside had padded partitions into which he placed the cameras and lenses.

'There's more.' He opened another of the red boxes and brought out five rolls of film. 'Kodak 2234. If you're shooting the Dream lens, you might as well use the sharpest film that there is. Shoot it at ISO 50 and tell Dwarkanath.'

I picked up the valise and walked back towards Hillcrest.

I was barely through the door when my phone rang. It was an unfamiliar number.

'Hello'?

'Mr Arya?' someone with an American accent.

'Yes, this is Harish.'

'Mr Arya, my name is Angad Bhullar. I'm a solicitor engaged by Global Affairs Canada.'

Ah, Canadian surd.

'Hello Angad…' My phone beeped. It was Shankar, my criminal lawyer also trying to reach me. Two lawyers trying to speak to me at the same time—this must be special. 'Sorry, I was distracted by the other line. So how may I help you?'

'Mr Arya, this pertains to your petition against the Canadian Government alleging complicity in the parental abduction of your daughter Srishti Arya by your estranged wife Sameera Sethi.'

'Go on,' was the best I could say.

'Mr Arya, would it be possible for us to meet today to discuss this? There seem to be some gaps in the Canadian Government's view of this matter and the specific assertions made in the petition. I'm hoping that we can clear this thing up at the earliest.'

'Mr Bhullar, I'm travelling at the moment, I'm expecting to be back in Delhi sometime next week. Perhaps we could meet then.'

'Mr Arya, I wouldn't insist if this wasn't important, but at about 3 am today Ms Arya and Ms Sethi were detained by Indian immigration officers while departing for Canada. They're currently in detention at the airport hotel.'

'What?'

'Mr Arya, please make it convenient for us to meet

and resolve this as soon as possible. Srishti is currently in detention—under armed guard at the Airport hotel.'

'Have you spoken with my lawyer?'

'No sir. I thought it would be best to speak to you first.'

'I shall return to Delhi as soon as I can but please direct all further communication to my lawyer.'

'Certainly Mr Arya.'

'My lawyer will be in touch when I'm back in town.'

I called Shankar back.

'Darbari fucked them!' Shankar screamed. 'He's fucked the former Canadian Ambassador, the Canadian Foreign Minister, the Canadian Embassy in India, he's fucked everybody. Now they just have to come to the table and talk.'

'Calm down Shankar. What do we need to do?'

'We need to meet Darbari and move further.' So obviously Shankar didn't have a clue.

'OK. Let me speak to him.'

I phoned Darbari, but he didn't take my call.

I drove as fast as I could to Baxter Lodge and rushed through the door. Chaaya was dealing with a guest in the lobby and noted my presence. As soon as the guest left, I walked briskly towards her. She motioned to her office.

Once in, she closed the door and folded her arms—a light smile played on her lips.

'Looks like Darbari has come through,' I gushed. 'Sameera and Srishti were detained by Immigration this morning. I'm driving back to Delhi.'

'Let me see if I can save you the drive.'

She picked up her desk phone and punched in four digits.

She had a fifteen second conversation in Japanese and disconnected.

'Fly out on the chopper at 3 pm,' she said to me.

I drove back to Hillcrest and packed a bag. On second thought, I took the camera valise along.

I walked into Darbari's study at 6 pm. He was at his desk, arms folded, looking very pleased with himself.

'Good evening, Harish. That was quite fast.'

'Good evening, Sir. Yes, I was lucky to be able to fly.'

He raised his eyebrows in apparent surprise. 'Should we go meet the Canadians?'

'What about Srishti?'

'I spoke to the hotel and the Airport Police. They shifted them to a suite which you'll be paying for if Sameera or the Canadians don't. They're comfortable for now. They have a lawyer trying to secure their release, which will not happen in a rush because of multiple issues involved here.'

Darbari got on the phone with who I assumed was Angad Bhullar and agreed to meet him in forty-five minutes. We got into Darbari's Volkswagen and drove to the Central Delhi office of a well-known law firm. The meeting was held in a conference room three floors underground.

Bhullar was accompanied by an Indian lawyer—Parizaad Vakil. Vakil and Darbari seemed to be cut from the same cloth. Over four hours, they took apart the entire situation piece by piece—Darbari passing sheets of paper from his briefcase to Vakil who speed read them and put them in a pile beside her. Bhullar's eyes had glassed over at about the 30-minute mark.

Vakil had very few questions. When she was done, Darbari shut his briefcase delicately and looked Vakil in the eye.

'At the end of it, Counsellor Vakil, my client is not here for revenge—though his estranged wife and the Canadian Government have given him enough cause to desire such. All he wants is a place in his daughter's life.'

'Compensation?' she asked.

'Nothing outside of his legal fees for the abduction matter. He will bear the fees for the marital matter himself.'

Vakil swivelled to look at Bhullar who was asleep with his eyes open. Ask any litigation counsel, that really is a thing.

'There is the matter that both mother and child are Canadian citizens.'

'Only on paper,' Darbari said. 'It's quite clear that the mother has lived here for two years prior to her marriage and the child had lived here her entire life until the abduction. Under the Hague convention, that determines Gurgaon, India as having been her place of habitual residence.'

'It could be argued,' Vakil said thoughtfully, 'that life in Canada would offer greater security, opportunity, and enrichment to the child.'

'Which my client is not disputing. He is a financially comfortable entrepreneur who had a fabulous career ahead of him until the false criminal cases ran him into the ground. The mother's family lives in a seven-million-dollar home in the heart of New Delhi and has substantial assets and income. Between the two of them they could afford the finest schools and experiences for Srishti. And Counsellor Vakil, my opinion is, and I'm sure you will agree, that the affection of two involved parents is no substitute for any number of fancy schools or stimulating experiences.'

'How do you want to do this?' she asked.

'Under the principle of the Right to Access, suspend their passports until the custody agreement is signed. Draw up the settlement agreement between my client and the Canadian government on the basis of what we discussed. My client has no desire to engage in a protracted litigation with anyone.' He cleared his throat and added some more mettle to his voice. 'Provided there's no further interference in his parental rights in the frenzy of misguided righteousness.'

Vakil smiled. 'I'll work on that Counsellor. I'll phone your office to schedule a review meeting.'

'Oh, Counsellor please—' Darbari slid his card across the table, 'phone me.'

It was 1 am when we left the office. I summoned an Uber.

'When do I get to see Srishti?'

Darbari turned to me with a smile. 'I told you that Sameera would bring Srishti to you.'

'When?'

'Get home, get some sleep, get up, and get pretty. She'll call.'

My Uber arrived.

I did just what Darbari said.

At 11 am I got a call from a foreign number.

'Hello?'

'Harish. Sameera here.'

My heart started thudding and my body started trembling. I couldn't help it. Tears started streaming down my face, and I started sobbing. In that moment, I think my heart broke.

'Why did this happen to us?' I sobbed.

There was only silence from the other end.

'Are you there?' I asked.

'Yes.' It sounded as if she had been crying too. 'I want us to meet.'

'I want to see Srishti.' I sobbed.

'Yes. You will. But I want to talk to you first. It's going to be a little awkward, because whatever demon you have brought from hell to do this to us has a woman with a gun standing outside our door.' She still had her way with words.

'I'm coming to the hotel. Let me see what I can do.'

'Just you. I don't want to talk to a lawyer right now.'

'Just me.'

I phoned Darbari about the conversation and got an Uber.

It was as if all the anguish from the past two years had been waiting for that moment to burst forward. I was trembling, sweating—holding back tears on the ride to the Airport. Darbari arrived at the hotel just a few seconds after me.

As I walked through the hotel lobby with Bunky pressed to my chest, I noticed Sameera's father lurking in the coffee shop with murder in his eyes. Sunny was there too, in a chair at the reception. He seemed to be checking in.

Darbari made a phone call. A policeman appeared and led me to one of the conference rooms.

There she was. A policewoman who was in the room with her left.

Exactly the way I remembered her. Exactly the way she looked sitting at the breakfast table that morning that I left home for my office—and returned to an empty flat.

I sat down.

'Hi,' she said. Her eyes were red—she had been crying.

'Hi,' my voice trembled.

It was a silent minute. Perhaps it was just ten seconds, perhaps it was just ten minutes. I had rehearsed this moment for two years now. I had speeches I could make—venomous ones, grovelling ones, even a businesslike proposal, but words failed me.

'So, what now?' she asked.

'Let's begin with the why,' I said.

Sameera threw her head back and wiped a tear from the corner of her left eye. 'It feels like a different lifetime. I don't even remember much.'

'What do you remember?'

'Being sad. Disappointed. Betrayed even.'

'Why?'

'Everything changed. Do you know how much I had to fight to marry you? And why did I do so? You were full of passion. Knowledge. Every night you came home to me felt like a gift. But then things began to change. There were times when you would just see through me. I thought it would get better when Srishti was born, but no, it got worse.' She wiped another tear from her eye.

'The night before I left, you were pacing in the living room, speaking on the phone to some Bhalla guy. Srishti followed you with her eyes twinkling. She walked behind you—holding her hand out—trying to reach you. You didn't even notice. She called for you loudly. You made a face, walked out of the room, and slammed the door. She was disappointed when she walked to me, and though I held her for two hours, she wouldn't stop calling for you. You finally came to the dinner table in a foul mood and didn't even acknowledge her presence as she tried to speak to you. I know men like that. I've seen many men like that. They raise broken children. They raise women who would do the most desperate things for a man's attention and men who do the most reckless things to get a reaction out of other men.'

My face was on fire. My nostrils were flaring. Boiling tears were rolling down my face.

Sameera continued. 'I thought I would leave for a few days and return when you had a chance to think things over. But then I saw how my parents and cousins doted over Srishti. She walked around the house like a princess. That's when I realised what an island of selfishness you had become. I decided that I deserved better. I decided not to come back.'

I broke down. I may have cried for a good five minutes while she watched me in silence.

'I'm going to let you meet Srishti,' she said. 'I'm going to give you space in her life. But remember—if you ever sow the slightest seed of doubt in her mind—do anything at all that will make her think any less of me as a mother, I will fucking kill you. I will fucking cut up your face and shoot you in the head. This is India—money and connections can get me out of anything. Right now, my father is on the phone to the Home Ministry. Suhani is on her honeymoon, but her husband is talking to External Affairs. Someone is probably on his way to a Supreme Court Judge's house to get an emergency order.

Srishti and I will be home by 5.'

'Why the criminal cases?' I asked.

'That wasn't me. That was my dad's idea. When I mentioned the cases to the Canadian Embassy, they just ran with it.'

'Can I see Srishti?'

'Go wash your face.'

I left the conference room and washed my face in the men's room. Darbari came up beside me and quietly gave me a splash of Yardley Gold.

When I re-entered the room, Sameera was there with Srishti. Srishti was sitting on the edge of her chair, swinging her legs. She looked me in the eye.

'Srishti, baby, your daddy is here,' Sameera said.

'Hi,' Srishti said.

I sat down beside her. 'Hi Srishti. Do you remember me?'

She pushed all the way back in her chair and nodded, but seemed unsure.

'Srishti, do you remember Bunky?' I put the purple monkey on the table in front of her.

She grabbed him and hugged him to her shoulder just as she did when she was a baby. 'Hi Bunky,' she murmured. She had a Canadian accent. She looked up at me. 'If you're my daddy, why aren't you with us?'

I could feel Sameera glaring at me in warning.

'It's my fault baby; I didn't come with you. But I'm

sorry. I'm really sorry. Can I be with you now?'

'Why didn't you come with us?'

'I don't know Srishti. I don't have an answer for you.'

'But why?'

There was nothing for me but the refuge of silence.

'OK,' Srishti said. 'You can come with us.' She turned to Sameera. 'Daddy is going to come with us.'

'He can't come with us right now Srishti.'

'Why?'

'You remember the police officer lady outside our room? She won't let him come inside.'

'I'll talk to her,' Srishti said. 'Off-ic-er Lata Aunty!' Srishti called loudly in an accented sing-song.

The door opened and a severe looking policewoman with a service pistol at her hip stepped in.

'Yes baby?'

Srishti pointed to me. 'This is my daddy.' She pointed to the lady officer. 'This is my Police Officer Lata Aunty. My daddy is coming with me.'

Officer Lata looked at Sameera, who nodded ever so slightly. Then she looked at me with flamethrower eyes. She nodded. 'OK baby.'

'See, he can come with us. And then we can go home and meet everyone.'

'He won't come home with us today, Srish, but you can go meet him all day on Sunday.'

Srishti seemed a bit disappointed. 'Sunday? Promise?'

'Yes. Promise,' she said.

We left the conference room and went up to the suite. We ordered lunch. Sameera had pasta, Srishti had parts of a fruit salad, some French fries, and half a chicken sandwich. I had a margherita pizza and a coke. I listened to Srishti tell me about her school, their neighbour's dog called Trudeau, and about Suhani's wedding.

Just as Sameera had predicted, at 4 pm a lawyer walked to the police officers outside the suite and gave them copies of a court order. Sunny and Sameera's father entered the suite, and after very perfunctory comments to me, escorted them out. Darbari stood just outside the door watching all of this.

'Well, at least you don't have to pay me the first half of my fee.' He spun around and did a bit of a dance walk to the lifts.

Over the next few days, we hammered out the custody and support agreement. Sameera agreed to stay in India. We would get Srishti into a school in Delhi, and I would have weekend visitation.

Chapter 13

I had Hiroto's proposal in mind. I gathered as much information as I could about Linguintel. GK had been quite active building the company's brand. He had a couple of TEDx talks, a few of the IT team had been very active on the tech forums, and the company had filed over 38 patents since I had left.

I met Hiroto at his Delhi apartment. I had prepared a presentation on the company's current state as I saw it, and how I could build it out to align with what Hiroto had in mind. He waited through it patiently, asked a few general questions.

He invited me to move to the bar. I hadn't touched alcohol since that night at Baxterpur, so I took a bottle of ginger ale. He did the same.

'You'll have to forgive me,' he said. 'I haven't really given you the substance of my vision. You may think this acquisition is a financial investment, but it is not. It's a functional part of a much larger strategy that Sogacorp has been working on since 1949.

It's a very bold vision—the sort technology industry has pushed for the last fifty years. Convergence, convenience, upliftment, communication, sustainability, efficiency...all strong words, bold words, but everything that they have achieved so far has been the opposite. This individualism nonsense has blown into selfishness. The world these players operate in is a zero-sum game—winner takes all. One wins; everyone else loses.

'And the collectivists? Rabid, identity-centric lunatics—also playing a zero-sum game. They want to pull down every traditional structure in society claiming that they're evil, steeped in violence and injustice—yet don't have a viable structure as an alternative. You see, the free market in its truest form, socialism in its truest form, anarchism in its truest form—are all perfect systems, if, and this is a big if—they are underscored by integrity, compassion, and unity.

'That's what I want to build—something rooted in integrity, compassion, and unity. Like the Indian scriptures say: Vasudhaiva Kutumbakam—the world as one family. Incidentally, this concept has found its way into Shintoism—my family's faith.

'But, in recorded history, we have seen empires rise and fall. Entire civilizations rise from riverbeds, seashores, desert oases, or mountaintops. They build prosperity, wealth, knowledge, art—a period of great wellbeing—until some oaf comes along with a zero-sum plan to conquer the world, or some such scheme. Corrupt, brutish, and greedy enablers help him squander a century's progress in a decade or two. And then we're back to square one.

'My family's been a part of this three times in the past eight hundred years. I was fortunate to go to Eton and read history at Oxford, and I saw how this pattern repeated itself—scores of times—throughout the unhappy history of our species.

'This time, I believe, things could be different. Humanism has changed humanity so that we share a somewhat common idea of what is right and wrong. Of course, we let it be coloured by our own petty prejudices. But we have the means to organise, like never before, and we have the fiction of global finance.'

'The fiction of global finance?' I wondered where he was going with this.

'Yes—money printing. After the Second World War, the United States emerged as a global leader, superseding the British empire. Thanks to the Marshall Plan, Europe was awash in US Dollars—which became the default global currency.

'The dollar's value was tied to the value of gold—a rare, finite metal mined in small quantities. This created a problem, as all the finance tycoons needed money to multiply money. The more money you have—the more you could risk—and the more money you could take home. The problem was the money supply was limited to how quickly governments could acquire gold.

'In 1971, Richard Nixon ended the Bretton Woods system that pegged all major global currencies to gold. After that, anyone could print as much money as they liked. As long as everyone printed money at around the same rate, balance was maintained—unless of course, you're Mozambique and you go completely bonkers.

'So, what do we get—yearly GDP growth of 7%, 8%—20% and upwards in unregulated economies where resources can be plundered. All of it propped up by US dollars that have no real backing. The money in supply moves from the public balance sheet to private assets in a couple of quarters.'

'I really don't understand this.'

'Okay—suppose I own a shoe company. I invest my savings in a workshop, and earn 20% profit. Then I walk into Sumitomo and get a million-dollar loan at 7%, I increase my output which in turn increases my margin to 25%—and in that year, I make a $250,000 profit. After I pay Sumitomo their $70,000—Sogashoes is left with a cash pile of $180,000.

'Next Sumitomo's General manager offers me ten million dollars. The next year, I increase my margin to 30% and make a $3 million profit. Sumitomo receives $700,000 in interest payments, and Sogashoes's cash pile rises by another $2.3 million. Then Sogashoes's investors clamour for a dividend because of the extra cash earned. The money borrowed from the bank is distributed to shareholders, and ends up in houses, cars—maybe a diamond necklace for the mistress.

'This continues with ever increasing sums of money until Bushidawalker and Adachistep hit the market with superior products and Sogashoes goes tits up. What do the banks do about the loan? They write it off. In developed economies they don't chase investors to return their dividends. In fact, the collectivists will protest at their local politician's home and the banks may even give Sogashoes more cash to stay afloat.

'When this happens to a thousand companies, and the banks have a bad loan crisis, the government steps in—prints $100 billion for a bailout—and business goes on as usual.'

'OK—like what the USA did in 2008,' I said.

'And 2002. Then in 1983, 1977, and in 1929...' He may have seen confusion on my face. He paused for a second and cleared his throat.

'Sorry—I have a point and I'm getting to it.'

'You may want to hurry,' I half-joked.

'We have been playing this system for the past fifty or so years. We have been borrowing from Japanese banks since 1948, and from British banks since 2008. Slow growth—nothing like the way startups rise. We borrow at about 3% and have a global margin of about 8%. There is the frequent money spinner among the businesses we own—and we've been very lucky with that, but we're generally conservative. Four hundred companies—a well-oiled machine, efficient, risk averse, and very well diversified.

'Within Japan, we have family-managed organic tofu companies, sake breweries, noodle factories, industrial supply chains, profitable real estate, shipping companies, agricultural holdings—rice, timber, wasabi, and I'm only talking about Japan—where our focus is economic activity.

'In Bangladesh we have the largest mail order pharmaceutical business on the planet—selling generic lifesaving drugs—insulin, statins, antihypertensives, antidepressants and such to Americans at a 5% margin.

'In India, Sogacorp companies own vast swathes of wasteland—bought for a few dollars an acre. We are planting dense Miyawaki forests—fruit, fodder, and timber—harvestable in two decades. We are doing the same with several million acres across Saudi Arabia, Tanzania, Algeria, Tunisia, Egypt, Botswana, and South Africa. Once these forests grow dense, we will be the world's largest privately owned carbon fixer—the only one with any material impact on climate change. And wait till we start playing the carbon credit market once they force the Paris Agreement down everyone's throat.

'Amazing,' I said.

'We have our own research lab—rare metal recovery, plastic recycling, battery technology, efficient solar power, hundreds of circular economy projects. Four hundred scientists and inventors producing about two hundred patents a year.'

'Wow.'

'Our own consulting company, that works constantly to make these companies more efficient, our own airline, security corporation, hospitals across three continents, employee housing. You get the point I hope.'

'Somewhat, yes. But where does Linguintel come in?'

'This is where I want to drive social change. Getting people to actually talk to each other. Right now, in my head, it's a very nebulous concept that's just coming together. I want to bring it in. I want you to build what I asked—and then we'll toss it to the consulting company and see what they do with it.'

I thought for a few seconds, sipping my now warm ginger ale.

'OK. I'll do it.'

'I'm pleased to hear that.' He smiled. 'I offered Akshay Bhalla $100 million for Linguintel this afternoon.'

I nearly fell off the stool. 'They're not worth that!' I shouted—then checked myself and lowered my voice. 'Zero revenue. A minimum viable product that hasn't gained traction. You offered a hundred million dollars for that? You know Akshay Bhalla—he'll only bargain upwards!'

'Oh, don't worry about that.'

'Well, it's your money.'

'Dinner?'

'Good morning, Mr Arya, please hold for Mr Akshay Bhalla.'

Beep!

'Hello Harish.'

'Hi Akshay. How's it going?'

'It's been busy Harish. We need to speak. I would like you to join me for dinner this evening. I'll send my car for you at 7.30.'

'No Akshay. I'm busy for dinner. I can't do tonight,' I lied.

'Harish, I insist. There's a lot at stake; we have to meet tonight. I will be upset if you brush me off.'

'I'm not brushing you off Akshay. I have a life. I'm not one of your minions who's at your beck and call every time you snap your fingers. You can't call me at 11 am and demand my presence for dinner.'

Fucking asshole.

A long silence—

Then his tone changed.

'Either you meet me tonight, or Hejamady, Sunaina, Ritwick—your fabulous fourteen at Linguintel—will lose their buyouts. All of them. Not a paisa for sticking around for the three-year lock-in. I'm going to terminate all of them for underperformance.'

'You're threatening me? Really?'

'Yes.'

I gave in. 'I'll clear my calendar.'

'My car will pick you up at 7.'

I stepped out of the black Mercedes Maybach and walked towards the Antechamber to Hell. The bouncer looked at me, but I held him with a glare.

'Don't even think about it.' He hesitated for a second but then stepped forward—about to say something.

My peripheral vision caught some movement. Bushida and Adachi rose from a couch in the corner and started walking towards us in slow but confident strides.

'Hi guys!' I said in my brightest voice. Both of them nodded in response.

The bouncer backed off. The uniformed attendant led me to a dining room on the first floor. Akshay Bhalla sat at the table, with Hiroto opposite him. Hiroto stood up.

'Nice to see you, Harish!' Bhalla chimed, oozing South Delhi insincerity.

'I can't say the same given the manner in which I was persuaded. Nice car though—I've always wanted to see a Maybach on the inside.'

I turned to Hiroto. 'Hiroto san, konbanwa.' I bowed.

'Harish san, konbanwa.' He bowed.

'Well, now that we're done with the pleasantries,' Bhalla said, 'what are we going to drink? I have sake—Hakkisan, Junmai, Honjozo, Fukuju.'

Hiroto laughed. 'Sake is not consumed the way Indians drink Whiskey,' he said scornfully. 'The host considers the weather, the time of day, the occasion, how drunk he wants you to get, and what you will be eating. He serves what he wants to, and the guests drink with gratitude and no complaints.'

Bhalla thought for a second. 'Honjozo then.'

He squeezed the edge of the table and the attendant entered. He gave the man instructions in Hindi.

The drinks trolley appeared and the attendant poured out the sake into crystal shot glasses.

Hiroto raised his glass. 'To what we're about to discuss.'

Bhalla and I raised our glasses.

'Thank you for having me over,' said Hiroto. 'I thought this will be a discussion between just the two of us, but I'm pleased to see my friend Harish here.'

Bhalla smiled. 'Well, I received an acquisition offer for Linguintel from the deal team at Kusakabe-Courtenay's London office. Since both of you were in the same city, I thought I'd speak with you in person.'

'I see,' Hiroto said.

'To be honest Hiroto, it was a bit impersonal to hear from a Managing Director at an investment bank for a transaction this size.' Bhalla continued. 'It's always more tasteful for something this huge to begin as a meeting between equals.'

Well, I'm sorry if you're offended, Akshay,' Hiroto said.

'I'm not knowledgeable enough to discuss transactions. Kusakabe-Courtenay is the merchant bank that handles all my acquisitions. I just point at something and say—buy that—and they buy it! Then I go to someone like Harish and say—hey, I've bought this—now this is what I want done. That's it.'

'I am interested in the reasoning behind the valuation,' Akshay said.

'That's for the MD at Kusakabe-Courtenay to explain, but you know what these damn investment bankers are like—it's so hard to get anything intelligible out of them. It's really quite remarkable that I still have any money left after all the acquisitions in the past eighteen months.'

'Why do you want Linguintel?' Bhalla asked firmly.

'Now—that's a strategic matter for Sogacorp. I will not discuss that.'

'Hiroto, I'm going to propose something. You don't have to answer this right now, but think over it. How about we start a fund together—We seed it—let's say one billion each—and then go to Limited Partners to raise more. I'm telling you—with Shaybee's market access and your strategic view, we could easily raise a hundred-billion-dollar fund. Maybe even two hundred billion, five or six years down the line.'

Hiroto emptied his glass and brought it to the table with a sharp tap. 'I already am a two-hundred-billion-dollar fund. And the answer is—no.'

Bhalla's nostrils flared. His lips started twitching.

'Let me tell you why,' Hiroto said.

'We are very different people. I've followed your investments, your exits, the way you operate—it's a style that is the antithesis of Sogacorp. I wanted Linguintel, and I almost had it three years ago—Kusakabe-Courtenay didn't want to touch it because of the way you muddied the waters around it. What was the vision that you had for it? Where is it now? I don't understand it. We can never be business partners because I don't understand how you operate.'

'What makes you think that you'll get Linguintel now?'

'I am optimistic,' Hiroto said.

'I hear that the Canadian Pension Fund is suing Merrill Lynch and Blackrock over transparency and reporting related to investment performance. It is a government body and one of the largest investors in the world, so I expect the Securities and Exchange Commission will hire a specialist consultant to value their sub-mandates to funds like yours. That consultant needs to justify a fee. He will use a conservative valuation methodology lacking the exuberant assumptions that priced Uber at forty-one billion dollars. My guess is that they'll mark your portfolio down by between fifty and seventy per cent. Ten billion will drop to three billion in a blink.'

'That won't happen!' Bhalla spluttered.

'What then,' Hiroto continued, 'will your investors say, when they find out that you turned down a hundred million dollars in cash for a company that has no revenue and a product that still hasn't defined its market?'

Bhalla was fuming.

'I must now leave,' Hiroto said, rising from his seat. 'It's nearly dark and my men must eat. Come along Harish. I'll give you a ride.'

'Sit right there Harish, or the fabulous fourteen lose their buyout.'

I stood up, my heart pounding. 'It's just three million dollars in total,' I spluttered. 'I'll start a company called Languintel and hire them with a joining bonus.'

I followed Hiroto out.

Seeing us come down the stairs, Adachi jogged to the portico and brought around an SUV. Once inside, Hiroto issued instructions in Japanese. Bushida and Adachi responded with a crisp, 'Hai'.

'Take us to your home,' Adachi said.

I put on my Google Maps and passed it to the front.

'No. No. I need my eyes on the road,' Adachi snapped. 'Give me precise directions as we drive.'

We got home.

'Hurry,' Bushida said. 'Pack a bag and get down here.'

'Why?'

'Please do as he says,' Hiroto urged. It was the first time ever that I had heard a tinge of anxiety in his voice.

I shrugged. I went up to the flat, packed an overnight bag with some underwear, a few T-shirts and a pair of jeans. Laptops, phones, chargers, disk drives. I picked up the camera bag on my way out. Once back in the car, I realised that I had forgotten socks, my toothbrush, and my shaving kit.

'You're not going to be back here for a few days,' Hiroto said. 'If you're missing anything, we'll get it for you at my place.'

We sped from Gurgaon back into Delhi.

'Does that thug really think he is my equal?' Hiroto raged. 'I'm sorry Harish. I let my pride get the better of me and I may have put you in danger.'

'Don't worry. It had to be said.'

'You're going to stay with me until Bhalla makes his next move. Adachi will drive you anywhere you need to go.'

We reached Hiroto's apartment.

'Sake.' Hiroto huffed just as we got through the door. He plonked down on the couch in the living room. Bushida went to the bar and brought out a bottle and four cups.

'You'll have to excuse me, Harish,' Hiroto said, 'like all polyglots I'm going to retreat to the comfort of my native tongue in this hour of anxiety.'

'Not a problem, I said.'

He took a shot of sake and Bushida refilled his cup.

Hiroto then acted out the meeting in Japanese—switching voices for each part. Bhalla was a brooding hunchback who spoke in a sinister throaty drawl. I was an inexpressive statue with soft words. Hiroto himself was a majestic postured hero with a deep voice and measured tone. He took a sip of sake each time he switched character—Bushida kept it coming.

Adachi and Bushida laughed and cheered him on in Japanese.

When he got to what I think was my parting shot—I distinctly heard 'Langruintelu' in there—they jumped up with a cheer and Adachi thumped my back.

Hiroto dropped to the carpet and caught his breath. 'That's how all Japanese folk tales were created and passed down.' He panted.

'What a pretentious boor. 'Hakkisan, Junmai, Honjozo,' he recited mockingly—reverting to Bhalla voice from a few moments earlier. You're good though—Hiroto san, Konbanwa—I should send you to a Yose coach when you come to Nara.'

'So, this is how Hiroto Soga unwinds,' I remarked.

'Yes.' He took another sip of sake. 'Everyone needs the kind of friends you can be the jester with. Otherwise, life gets too serious! I can't keep my BBC Money manners all the time. It would be dreadful! The three of us have known each other since we were children in Nara. My father would have loved for me to get involved with Kendo and Jujitsu like these two did—the proper training for a Soga child, but I was totally enamoured by the Yose and Kabuki troupes that visited Nara and we always went to watch them. Bushida, remember the time my grandfather caught me putting on my grandmother's makeup?'

The mirth drained from Bushida's face in an instant. He retorted gruffly in Japanese.

Hiroto laughed. 'I did lines from Yoshitsune as he beat me—with full expression and everything.'

He smiled wistfully. 'Yoshitsune Senbon Sakura is to Kabuki what the Scottish Play is to Western theatre. My grandfather beat me with a Kendo stick because I used my grandmother's makeup. Bushida was there—he doesn't find it funny. Forty-five years have passed and he still doesn't find it funny.'

He paused for a moment. 'Let's take a photograph.'

Adachi brought out the camera and the tripod. He set it up in a corner of the room and focused it. He set the timer and ran over to where we were seated. He was smartly in position when the shutter clicked.

The ground and first floors of the building where Hiroto stayed were occupied by the family of a British diplomat. They had twin daughters—Eva and Clara—four years old. In the mornings, when Hiroto, Bushida, and Adachi exercised on the roof, the girls were up there with their Indian nanny—counting reps in Japanese. Forty-five years, Hiroto had said. That placed the three of them in their early fifties. They did some pretty impressive bodyweight stuff—lots of pushups, pullups, squats, some jujitsu play-fighting, kendo—even some Aikido that the girls imitated.

What really caught my attention was a wooden board wrapped in some sort of rope. Bushida and Adachi took turns punching it. Adachi told me it was a makiwara—a tool used to condition fists. A hundred thousand punches, and you get fists of cedar. One million punches, and you get fists of stone. One million punches—that's a hundred punches each and every day for 28 years.

They did about an hour of intense exercise each day, ate a light breakfast, and retreated to their rooms. I would hear them talking on their phones in English and Japanese. Adachi would come out in the evenings and sit on the stairs with Eva, Clara, and their nanny. The girls seemed to have picked up some spoken Japanese, and rhymes—that they would recite loudly on loop. Dinners were the usual Hiroto style—sitting around chatting, cooking in turns, no alcohol usually. The whole setup had the feel of a really posh boys' dorm with six Samurai Swords as a centre piece.

I kept myself busy with the plan that I was working on for Linguintel and reading something from the impressive library that Hiroto had assembled in the house.

That Sunday, Adachi drove me to Sameera's house. I spent the morning with Srishti. She had taken to Bunky quite well, and he was back under his napkin-blanket napping on her bed. Srishti told me how much she missed her school and her friends back in Canada. I wondered if keeping her in India would really be the best thing for her. This was something that Sameera and I needed to discuss.

She was happy though, surrounded by her extended family.

I took a picture of her on the Canon.

Sameera asked me if I wanted to go out for lunch. We never really had the chance to speak being always surrounded by lawyers, family, or Srishti. I agreed.

Adachi drove us to an Italian restaurant that we used to frequent when we were married. It felt awkward being back there, but it made talking easier, because we seemed to slip into a sense of familiarity and the corrosive mist of anger, awkwardness, and hurt that lingered over all our recent interactions seemed to dissipate.

'Why do you have a Japanese driver and a car with a British High Commission Number?' she asked me after a thoughtful sip of Pinot Grigio.

'He's not my driver. It's complicated.'

'Ufff—don't your complications ever end?'

'Well, just think of it as an employment benefit.'

Sameera laughed. She had always been easy to amuse. 'Do you get a Korean boy band for entertainment?'

Not yet. I'm looking to start my next venture, and a Japanese investor is on board.

'The start of another descent for you. I think our marriage went downhill when you got your investor on board for Linguintel.'

I took a few seconds to let her words sink in.

'You're giving me too much credit. Whatever caused our unhappiness came from within me.'

She seemed amused. 'Really?'

Since selling Linguintel I've been able to do a lot of thinking and reflection. I think we find a lot of space for deeper things when the shallow preoccupations of a livelihood are lifted. I've been spending a lot of time in Uttarakhand and have had the chance to think about a lot of stuff.

'Ah, I wondered.' She paused thoughtfully and her amusement blossomed into a toothy smile. 'You startup bros cash out, go to the hills, embrace Buddhism, and eventually turn into Naval Ravikant.'

I decided not to tell her about the monk.

'Well, perhaps all of us take a similar path to comfort. Growing up in the 1990s was hard, even if you were what we called middle class. When you exit, there's money in the bank. You don't need to worry about where your next meal is coming from, and in fact if you're careful, you don't need to worry about your next meal for three hundred years. You don't need to go drinking with the VCs so you don't need to be in Delhi. Your phone calls are only people asking you for money, so you don't even need to be in a place with cellular coverage. So, you go to the mountains for peace, and your mind fills with all the things that you missed out on when survival was a priority.'

'Is that why you came after us?'

'I don't know.'

Our salads arrived.

'Are you seeing anyone?' she asked.

'Is it important?'

Her face tightened and she immediately became serious. 'Yes. If you want access to Srishti, if Srishti is to spend time with you, it is important that this woman is a good influence. I don't want her to compete with me for Srishti. I don't want her to claim my child in any way. At some point I'll want to meet her and get to know her so that I can be assured that my daughter is safe.'

'That's fair. What about you?'

'Well, nothing serious thus far. I've just been taking the time to enjoy Srishti's precocious years.'

'I'm sorry for everything,' I said. 'Though nothing that I can ever say or do will be enough.'

'It's alright. We're here now. Just don't be a dick and make sure that Srishti doesn't miss having a father.'

On the drive back, Adachi seemed to take a longer route than necessary. I asked him if he needed help.

'We're being followed. Grey van.'

I looked through the rear windscreen. There was a grey van about two cars behind us.

'Amateurs.' Adachi muttered.

We reached home and Adachi jumped out of the car to pull the metal gates shut. I grabbed a chair from the watchman's cabin and climbed it to look over the top. Surely amateurs. They had pulled up right across the road from the gate. I still had the camera on me. I took a picture.

Adachi helped me down. 'Unnecessary,' he said, and pointed to the CCTV camera mounted on the gatepost.

That evening, four men from the British High Commission came to the apartment and swept it for hidden cameras and microphones. They found nothing. They even checked the Land Cruiser that we took that day. Nothing.

Chapter 14

That night, I revisited the routine monotony of Jaydip's life. It had completely dropped off my radar, neglected in the swirl of other things going on.

I flew to Bangalore.

I went back to Jaydip's office and retrieved the tracker from the car. I watched him get his coffee, then returned to my hotel room and destroyed the device.

The next day, I waited at the bar keeping an eye on the cafe. At 3.36 pm, he went in to get his coffee. I stood up and walked to the entrance of the bar for a better look. You know what they say—if you look hard at someone, they can feel your eyes? It's true.

As he left the coffee shop, I stared hard at the side of his head from a good forty feet away. He took maybe seven steps, slowed down, and looked around. His eyes swept past me—he froze and then looked straight at me. We stared at each other for about five seconds—then he dropped his gaze and took limp steps towards the lift.

I returned to my table. Thirty seconds later, he sat down on the chair across me and placed his takeaway cup on the table.

A server walked up to us. 'Sir, no outside foo—' His expression softened with recognition. 'Sorry sir.' He began to walk away.

'No, wait.' Jaydip held out the cup. 'Throw it away.'

The server hesitated 'No sir, it's…'

'I don't want it anymore. Throw it away. Bring me a cappuccino.'

The server took the cup from him and retreated into the kitchen.

Jaydip took a deep breath and exhaled. 'So, you finally got here.'

I didn't respond.

He looked from side-to-side—his head was trembling. 'Linguistic intelligence succeeded. You know, I have a Google alert for Linguintel? The fundraises, the acquisition, the new superstar CEO—I know all about it. I was beginning to think that it would all just fade away.'

He fell silent.

He made a couple of false starts before being able to speak. 'It was meant to be a joke. I was a dumb college kid with plenty of issues and no sense of consequences. I had a rough life—had been slogging my ass to get into the IITs from the 8th standard. Do you know that? I had no hobbies, enthusiasm, or leisure—just endless cramming for that one exam. And you know what? I didn't get in.

'Instead, I ended up in this shithole donation college in rural Karnataka. And Puran? This kid from back of beyond—some village in Bihar—comes up as the fucking superstar—literally teaching our professors.

'Do you know that dimwit structural physics lecturer of ours—what was his name…' He closed his eyes for a second and snapped his fingers. 'Ranganathan. Yes, Ranganathan. He used to call Puran home and learn from him—then teach the same damn thing in class to us the next day. I was jealous. I was angry. He was everything I wasn't. The only thing I could genuinely loathe in him was his personality.

'You remember what the college was like—the gangs. How did he even survive there? Just because he was helping the fourth years with their exams and projects, all four unions protected him. But they were the ones who enjoyed the '*Adventures of Puran*' the most—all those secretaries, treasurers, union presidents—the dregs of the system. They were the ones who enjoyed it the most.

'Was it really a crime? Tell me. Writing a comic strip. Who knew that he'd go and *hang* himself? Anywhere in the world, it would've been considered free speech.'

'Salacious libel and abetment to suicide,' I said softly.

Jaydip took a laboured breath.

'I've been a good man. Coming from that shit hole

college, I worked hard. Twelve-hour days in shit jobs, CAT prep at night. Went to a top college for my MBA. Returned as a manager. I built teams, products, mentored my juniors—groomed hundreds of professionals now in top companies. I have seven hundred employees working for me today. They feed their families, send their children to good schools, drive cars, go on vacations to Goa and Thailand. Seven hundred families—seven hundred—who depend on me. And my family. I'm a family man. A wife, two kids—'

'And a mistress,' I said, softer than last time.

He fell silent again. His coffee arrived.

'So, what are you going to do?' he asked.

'I haven't decided,' I said.

We sat there looking at each other.

He took a sip of his coffee and winced. 'I couldn't have known that it would happen. I couldn't even imagine that it could happen. And Linguintel—,' he laughed.

'Linguintel. That day when you stood up on the common room table while gulping down a bottle of rum and announced that you were going to use Neural Networks to catch the author—we laughed at you. No one could believe that this second-year alcoholic could get anything done. No one—'

'Yet, here we are.'

He rolled one arm over the backrest of his chair and stared at the floor.

'It shouldn't have happened. I couldn't have known. It can't be my fault.'

He looked at me. I could see that he was no longer the man he was ten minutes ago. His eyes were wild and darting. His fingers were trembling. He hunched over with his legs shaking.

I stood up, stuck a two-thousand-rupee note under my half-empty lemon soda and left.

'I can pay for my coffee.' His weak voice faded into the rustle of the mall as I walked out of the bar.

Chapter 15

Back in Delhi, I slipped back into the gentle routine of Hiroto's household. Chaaya and I spoke every evening—I told her what I had been up to.

One evening, I had just settled in with a book when the twins squealed in delight on the stairs outside. Seconds later, the door opened to a large pink-skinned European-looking man, with a scruffy mop of pure white hair. He wore a wrinkled grey suit and white shirt and each twin clung to a leg.

The girls let go of his legs and announced in unison:

'We present to you Lord Harold Percival Henry Courtenay Hyphen Lambert.'

'Thank you, miladies,' the man replied in posh English and bowed. The girls curtsied and ran back down the stairs.

Hiroto emerged out of his room. He and Harold kissed.

'How are you Toto?' Harold asked.

'Just wonderful,' Hiroto replied.

Harold turned to me. 'You must be Harish.'

'That's right, Lord Courtenay.'

He laughed. 'Pfft! Little girls and their fantasies,' he said in a playful singsong. 'There is a Lord Courtenay, also from Eton—but I am not he.' We shook hands. 'I'm Mister Courtenay Hyphen Lambert, but for the sake of convenience, you may call me Harry.'

A man in a white chauffeur's uniform brought in two large suitcases. Adachi wheeled them towards Hiroto's room.

'It's been a long flight. I'll join you gents in a little while.'

We got together for drinks an hour later. From the conversation, I gathered Harry was a principal at Kusakabe-Courtenay—a rather senior one, judging by his name. He seemed dismayed when Hiroto told him about the meeting with Bhalla. Harry confirmed pretty much what Hiroto had told Bhalla about the pension fund lawsuit—except that he expected the drawdown on Shaybee to be closer to 90%.

Harry stayed for two days. During this time, we had some intense discussions on Linguintel, its intellectual property, and the staff I thought would be important to the company. It also became quite clear that he and Hiroto were a couple—and had probably been together for much of their adult lives.

Then the Canadian Pension Fund scandal broke.

Shaybee and two other Indian venture funds came under investigation. There was talk of a forensic audit. I could tell Hiroto was anxious.

One night, as we lounged around the living room, a loud crash echoed outside the building. Bushida jumped to his feet and turned on the television. There was the sound of men shouting—swearing in Hindi—and then a gunshot. Security camera feeds lit up the screen—the grey van from a few days earlier had come crashing through the gate.

Adachi's face twisted into a terrifying mask of rage. He grabbed a short-sword from the rack and bounded towards the door.

'Adachi, no!' Hiroto shouted a few words in Japanese. Adachi froze and looked back at Hiroto with pleading tears in his eyes.

Bushida and Hiroto grabbed short swords too. Adachi positioned himself right by the door, unsheathed his sword, and dropped the scabbard to the carpet. Bushida, his sword unsheathed, took a stance in the centre of the living room. Hiroto grabbed me by the collar and dragged me into the far corner. 'Stay here. Right here.' He unsheathed his sword, and took a stance at Bushida's side.

Someone was trying to break down the door.

Hiroto shouted to Adachi in Japanese.

Adachi waited for a pause between blows—then unlocked the door. With the next hit, the door swung open. A man in an orange T-Shirt and faded blue jeans stumbled into the room with a pistol in his hand.

Adachi's blade swished. He lunged at the man and struck his forehead with the sword's pommel. The man stumbled back into the hallway and started screaming.

A second man with a gun tried to enter, but Adachi kicked the door shut on his arm. When the man came through again, Adachi slashed him across the chest and kicked him out.

'Embassy security! Drop your weapons!' a British accent shouted on a megaphone.

With the door still open a few inches, I saw flashlights bouncing in the hallway—screaming, swearing in Hindi, and crying.

'I will not say this again,' the megaphone voice continued. 'You are on UK government property. Drop your weapons.'

Hiroto looked at me over his shoulder. 'British people—always so polite.'

A volley of muffled gunshots followed.

I heard boots—heaving, moaning, and dragging in the hallway—the crackle of walkie-talkies.

'Darcy, Bushy, this is Jim, the megaphone voice returned, 'My boys are coming through, so just take it easy, alright?'

All three men dropped their swords.

Four soldiers in battle dress and maroon berets entered through the door aiming submachine guns. They fanned out into the living room. 'Darcy, anyone else here?' asked one of them.

'No,' Adachi shouted. 'The girls. Where are the girls?' He sounded frantic.

The lead soldier tilted his head and activated the radio on his shoulder. 'Status check on the twins please. Over.'

The radio crackled. 'Seven reporting. They're alright. They were sleeping when it all started and were woken by the fireworks. I'm taking them down to the cellar until you chaps clean up there.'

Hiroto picked up his sword and gave orders in Japanese. The three of them sheathed their swords and dropped them onto a rug. Bushida took the long swords off the rack and added them to the pile. He rolled the rug into a bundle and tied it up with his belt.

Then I saw it—a severed hand by the door—still holding a pistol.

A fifth soldier entered the flat. 'There's a van outside. Grab what you want and move.'

'Don't forget your passport,' Hiroto told me.

I dashed to my room, stuffed my passport into my camera bag, and came right out. Bushida hoisted the bundle of swords onto his shoulder and we left the apartment.

Six attackers in all. Three dead, three seated on the lawn with the soldiers guarding them. Sirens wailed.

We got into a white Mercedes van and sped to the Japanese embassy. At the embassy a doctor examined us. Adachi took me to a consular officer who granted me a Japanese visa.

That night, we boarded the Sogacorp jet for Japan. At Kansai International two cars drove us to the Soga compound on the outskirts of Nara—a beautiful wood and stone house—the kind that I had only seen in movies. Adachi showed me to a room and gave me a cell phone and a laptop.

I called Sameera and recounted in detail about what had happened. Despite how outlandish this all sounded, she believed me. I spoke to Srishti too and promised her that I would be back to see her soon.

I checked the Indian news channels on YouTube and realised why Sameera believed me so easily. News vans were outside Hiroto's Delhi house, the UK High Commission, the Diplomatic Enclave's police station, and the All India Institute of Medical Sciences. A picture of Eva and Clara—possibly from the Nanny's social media account was being flashed on all channels. The narrative was that New Delhi had become so dangerous that gangs of armed robbers were emboldened to attack diplomats in their homes.

There was a knock on my door. Hiroto walked into the room and turned on the television. Bloomberg was running a report on the Canadian Pension Fund case.

We watched in silence as the newsreader described the lawsuit and the SEC investigation. The segment was followed by a panel discussion on transparency and reporting in investment management—though it rapidly switched to an exploration of why a pension fund should be investing in private equity.

'Harry spoke to Merrill Lynch,' Hiroto said. 'We'll get Linguintel for seventy-five million—cash.'

We gathered for dinner—noodle soup, grilled beef, and vegetables.

'I'm sorry Harish,' Hiroto said. 'It's been terrible. If anything had happened to you—to the twins—I never even imagined it would come to this.'

'It's alright. Someone had to stand up to him, but what now?'

'Let's stay here for a few days. I want the dust to settle before I do anything further.'

We ate in silence for a few minutes. Then Hiroto said, 'Maybe we should take a photograph. We made ....out alive.'

Adachi stood up from the table and brought out the camera. Then I noticed it—the tiny Dwidala Camera logo—right beside the lens. He used the self-timer again and got a picture of us. I went back to my room and brought the Canon P. I put it up on the bar counter and was able to get the image in focus.

The self-timer ran out and the shutter fired.

We continued with dinner.

'I'm curious Hiroto,' I asked. 'Of all the beautiful

places in the world, why Baxterpur?'

He put his chopsticks down. 'Some places in the world grow on you. Some people change everything for you in one short conversation. I first went to Baxterpur five years ago, looking for the Boadicea lily. Chaaya was working with Harry at KC's London office. My father had retired three years earlier, and I was struggling with the enormity of Sogacorp and the decisions that I had to take. The Baxter Lodge was an old and musty stately home then, but something about the place appealed to me—a sense of stability and calm—a building made of rock and timber—just like the one we're in right now. Completed in the same year that my family home was built. Colonel Baxter and my great-great grandfather were similar men, with similar lives. Both of them had a youth drenched in blood, a tragic middle age, and luckily—an old age of relative joy and comfort. Something about the place resonated with me. Maybe it was a chance to connect to a time in my own history while not in the shadow of my father. The place was losing money and the owners were looking to sell, so we bought it.

'It wasn't all about the building though. One day, while walking through Baxterpur market, I was drawn to a shop—the strangest shop in the world—a camera shop run by a Buddhist monk. He invited me to lunch and sold me a film camera.'

'Did you pay cash?'

'No! Funnily, he took my pocket digital camera in exchange. But some of the things he said to me helped me form a model for dealing with my challenges. Analogue—the human element of moving parts—robust, repairable, enduring. The human element mostly. There was something magical about the place. Every time I walked in, there were signs as if I was expected. That camera changed the way I—' He looked at my camera—still on the bar counter. He walked over and picked it up. He smiled, noticing the gold lotus bud motif, and set it down. 'Well, it changed the way that I see the world. I think you already know what I mean.'

'I do,' I said. 'I keep going back too—tied up a lot of loose ends.'

'Loose ends.' Hiroto seemed to be rolling those words over his tongue like one does with wine at a tasting. 'Loose ends. I don't think that explains it completely. At least not for me. What I've begun to think is—that there is destiny—something that you can't control—like me being born on this estate—and then there's opportunity, intent, and action. Then there's this world in chaos—everyone needs a model to bring things together. Everyone needs a place—a physical place to anchor intention, faith, and ambition. Perhaps that's why people go on pilgrimages.'

'So, you boys really took knives to a fucking gunfight,' a woman's voice spoke from behind me.

Adachi flinched. 'Not a knife, a Dotanuki

Wakizashi,' he said curtly.

'Tomayto Tomahto,' she retorted.

A large woman with curly bronze hair and hazel eyes walked up to the table.

'Rivkah Aronofsky,' Hiroto said. 'Sogacorp's head of security.'

Rivkah waved at me and settled on a stool by the bar from where she had a good view of the dinner table. 'At least now, can we talk about some serious safety training for the three of you?'

'Safety training!' Adachi scoffed, 'just say guns and Krav Maga.'

'Yes. A month on the mountain. Maybe two.' Rivkah tapped a box of Marlboro reds on the counter and lit a cigarette with a slender gold lighter.

Hiroto processed this for a few seconds and laughed. 'Becky, come on—so now I need to run Sogacorp *and* be a trained killer?'

Rivkah blew a plume of smoke towards the ceiling 'Of course! Isn't that the Soga family tradition for the past twelve hundred years? At least until your father.'

Hiroto winced.

'Won't you join us for dinner?' I asked her.

'Can't,' Rivkah said. 'I can't eat that *trayf.* None of that stuff is kosher—kosher as in Jewish food rules. Oh, but here's an apple.' She squashed out the cigarette into a sake cup and picked up an apple from a basket on the bar.

'Why didn't you come to the house?' Rivkah asked through a mouthful of apple.

Hiroto looked at her. 'It takes me a couple of days to prepare myself to face my father. Tell Mrs Fujiwara that I'll come to breakfast tomorrow.'

'How long will you be here?'

'I don't know. I may head up to the shrine for a few days.'

The next morning, we walked the short distance to the Soga mansion. The Soga compound was a sprawling meadow of perhaps five hundred acres. The mansion itself was a grand old building right in the centre. Several other smaller homes were built in the same style across the compound as well as two circular greenhouses. The rear of the compound was bordered by a dense forest.

Mrs Fujiwara met us at the door. She must have been about eighty, dressed for the nineteen fifties in a lime green dress, turtle rim glasses, and hair done in an elegant bouffant. She was feisty and spoke in rapid-fire Japanese—the total antithesis of how Bushida and Adachi carried themselves. She led us to a large dining table where an elderly lady and a uniformed maid were laying out breakfast. Mrs Fujiwara introduced us to the lady—who turned out to be Hiroto's mother, and twittered with the maid in Japanese. Satisfied with the maid's response, she pulled a tasselled cord in the corner of the room and a bell tinkled somewhere in the house.

'Senior Soga is on the way, so let's get ready for

breakfast,' Mrs Fujiwara said in English.

Hiroto's father walked into the room accompanied by another man of about the same age. Both men wore black jackets and striped trousers with white neckties. Come to think of it, that's how Hiroto, Adachi, and Bushida were dressed too.

'That's Kenji,' Mrs Fujiwara whispered to me. 'He is to Senior Soga what Bushida and Adachi are to Toto.'

We settled down for breakfast and I felt very self-conscious. Until now, it had been all dorm style eating at a kitchen bar, but this time it appeared as if it were breakfast with the Queen of England—porcelain, silver, teacups, and three types of forks. Everyone around the table had such refined manners—seemingly forged from years and years of practice—I felt small. I contented myself with a buttered bun, two fried eggs, and a cup of coffee because I didn't want to risk making a noise while cutting bacon on porcelain. Senior Soga appeared to be a pleasant man—slender and handsome, even at his age, with an air of warm benevolence. He spoke very little. All of the conversation was in Japanese between Mrs Soga, Hiroto, and Mrs Fujiwara. Adachi and Kenji were having a quiet side conversation that Senior Soga was observing quite intently.

The pressure of breakfast lifted.

'Let's finish our coffee on the patio,' Hiroto said to me. We walked out to a wooden patio that overlooked a beautiful garden. Mrs Fujiwara joined us, followed closely by the maid pushing a wooden service trolley.

Kenji, Bushida, and Adachi settled on stone benches in a corner of the garden.

'Don't be impressed by all this formality,' Mrs Fujiwara said to me. 'These upper-class Japanese are more British than the British.'

'The true knower of all things,' Hiroto laughed.

Mrs Fujiwara looked at him over her glasses.

'No, I mean that in a good way.' He turned to me. 'Mrs Fujiwara has been with Sogacorp since she was sixteen. She was a secretary when my grandfather ran the company, the office manager when my father ran the company, and now she just runs everything, because I'm useless.'

Mrs Fujiwara smiled coyly and tapped Hiroto's shoulder 'flatterer'. Her manner suddenly became more businesslike. 'So, dinner with your father. Do you want to do it tonight? Or do you want to draw out your suffering until your last day here?'

'Tonight. I want to go to the shrine in a couple of days.'

'OK. I'll call the Kannushi.' She turned to me. 'Kannushi—Shinto priest. The Soga family has a shrine at the old Soga fort in the forest. It's a bit of a walk, but you will enjoy it.'

'It's more than a bit of a walk,' Hiroto said. 'It's a four-day camping trip, complete with pooping in the bushes. Are you up for it?'

'The way you describe it—doesn't sound like fun, but I think the exercise would do me good.'

Mrs Fujiwara clapped her hands and jumped to her feet. 'Great! Four Kimonos then!' She left.

'Kimonos?'

'Yes. You cannot face the Kami in—' she surveyed me from head to toe with a raised eyebrow '—in Lacoste.'

Mrs Fujiwara left.

'What have I just got myself into?' I asked Hiroto.

'A bit of a walk—don't worry, Adachi and Bushida will be there. It will all be alright.'

We lounged around the house all day. I went for a walk on the grounds. The grass brushed against my legs with each step, a rhythmic swishing that was hypnotic and seemed to make the sun seep into my soul. I missed Chaaya. I missed Srishti. I missed Sameera.

I walked in wide circles around the house and a couple of the other buildings on the compound, and then made for the north fence that bordered the forest. The swishing grass seemed to propel me towards the fence like waves lift a surfer. The smell of the grass gave way to a heavy, earthy, woody aroma that could have been a man's cologne. The forest came into view. Beautiful old trees—gnarled, mossy, with large, protruding roots, like the Hollywood stereotype of an enchanted forest. Something like a magnet within the woods was pulling me—not a call—a pull—almost involuntary. I realised that I was not really walking by myself. I was weightless—my feet were skimming over the tips of the grass. It struck me that with one well-timed jump, I could be perched on the top beam of the five-foot wooden fence.

A brown horse with Adachi astride cut me off and reared. Kenji caught up on a black steed with white ankles.

'Turn around,' Adachi said.

'I was just going to the fence,' I said, unsure if I had broken any house rules.

'It's time for tea anyway, let's go back to the house.'

Something in his tone told me that I shouldn't argue. I stuck my hands in my pockets and turned around.

Kenji said something in Japanese, and Adachi responded. The two went back and forth a few times in what seemed like an argument that Kenji finally won.

'Were the trees calling you?' Adachi asked me.

I looked up at him. He was dead serious.

'Not calling,' I said to him, 'they were pulling me—that's what it felt like—pulling.'

The two men looked at each other.

'OK, back to the house now,' Adachi said, 'Do you want to ride?'

'I don't know how to ride a horse.'

'That's fine we'll walk.' Both of them dismounted.

I walked back to the house with Adachi and Kenji following close behind, leading their horses by the reins.

Closer to the edge of the garden, they pulled away

to the side of the house—perhaps to where the horses had been tethered.

A few minutes later, the two of them reappeared from the house. I had just about made myself comfortable on one of the stone benches. Kenji sat beside me and took out a packet of American Spirit cigarettes. He offered me one—which I accepted. He lit mine and then one for himself. He spoke through the smoke in Japanese. Adachi translated.

'Kenji apologises. He doesn't want you to think that we're rude.'

'That's alright,' I said with a smile. 'Thanks for the cigarette.'

Kenji had more to say.

'People have a lot to say about the forest. It's inhabited by Kami—supernatural forces. Each force has its motivations and outcomes. We can't call them good or evil—those are purely human concepts. A Kami is a force of nature—just like the sun, rain, a storm, a flood, or an earthquake. It is how it affects our lives that we perceive it. The Kami were pulling you to them. They have a reason. This forest was here before the Soga family built their first fort here over a thousand years ago. Since then, many men, women and children have been taken by the Kami.'

'They died?' I asked, quite intrigued.

'We don't know. Most of them were never seen again. The few that came back were profoundly changed. They would not fit in with the world as we know it. In the West, people would call them insane—but maybe the Kami taught them something that changed their existence—but the consequence in this world—the human world—was all bad. I hope you understand why we stopped you.'

'I do. Thank you.'

Bushida came to where we were seated.

'Hiroto asked if you would like to join him in the greenhouse.'

The way he said it—was clear—there was only one answer to that question.

Bushida escorted me to one of the greenhouses on the property. Hiroto was in there, wearing an apron over his suit, holding a short santoku knife. When he saw me, he put the knife on a table.

'Thanks for joining me, come this way.'

We walked into one of the inner chambers of the greenhouse. At the far end, was the Boadicea lily in a large earthen pot, with the Sentinel orchids growing on a lattice arch above.

'You were right,' Hiroto said. We grew the Sentinel orchids, and were able to get the Boadicea bulbs to sprout and thrive. I looked around. This section of the greenhouse had scores of plants.

'All of these are psychoactive,' Hiroto said. 'They seemed to mark a turning point in the civilizations that used them.'

'Really now.'

I'm serious. In South America for instance, psychedelics pushed communities away from warfare and other brutish pursuits, and drove them to construct cities and buildings that have endured for over two thousand years.'

'Oh, come on. Everyone knows about the Aztecs and their human sacrifices.'

'Well, it can be argued that we know of these incidents only through the Spaniards. They could have fabricated these tales to claim that these people were worthy candidates for violent conversion to Catholicism. Which is what they actually did. They plundered the Mesoamerican civilizations, outlawed Ayahuasca, Peyote, and other such psychedelics, they destroyed all books and written records.'

'Oh, come on.'

'I'm quite serious. Look at India. Where are the books and writings of the Thomasine Christians from Southern India? They are the only unbroken tradition of Christianity that goes back to Christ, instead they too have been subsumed by European Catholicism with their cherry-picked lore.'

'This sounds depressing.'

'It is, when you think about it. Human progress is forever being reversed by human brutishness. Look at South America over seven thousand years of civilization—cities, religions, buildings, a celestial map that was accurate by 20th century standards, a calendar that is far superior to our bastard lunisolar calendar that's been adjusted by everyone from the Romans to the British Weather Office. All of this lost because Christian extremists funded by wealthy merchants landed there to pillage, loot, and convert. The Incas, for instance, stored information on knotted strings, with three basic knots. These knots were combined to represent sounds, words, and numbers. Imagine the mental capabilities that this civilization had? Literally to base an entire script on just three characters? The first thing the Conquistadores did was to kill all the shamans and scribes.'

'Really?'

'Yes. Everywhere in history, humans have shown dominance by destroying temples and books. Somehow, when a civilization begins to move away from the preoccupations of survival, and begin to explore science, the universe, and consciousness, the brutes show up and kill everyone. Here in Japan, the Heian period saw the birth of Japanese literature, the Haiku, and everything you know about Japanese workmanship and aesthetics. How did it end? A Samurai clan showed up and killed everybody. What followed was two hundred years of bloodshed, with the Kamakura Shogunate. The same thing has played out in Ancient Greece, the Roman Empire, Arabia, India, South-East Asia.'

I had to bring Hiroto's rambling to a point somehow. 'So what do these lilies mean to you?'

He stuck his hands into his pockets and seemed to ponder his toes. 'A new world.'

He looked at me with a sort of warm intensity. 'I discovered these plants when reading books from my grandmother's collection. I think that exploring the dimensions of time, space, and consciousness are important for all human beings, and perhaps these plants hold the key to this. James Crick was supposed to be high on LSD when he postulated the helical structure of DNA. Aldous Huxley documented his experience with Mescaline in, 'The Doors of Perception'. However, these substances are banned in almost every country that calls itself civilized, and even possession is punishable with severe imprisonment and even death. One would think that brutes in suits don't want their subjects to broaden their consciousness and open the doors of perception.'

'Drugs can be addictive—if everyone was high, society would collapse. Perhaps that's what happened to these civilizations that were felled by brutes.'

'Yes, certain drugs are addictive—Heroin, Cocaine, Alcohol, Caffeine too. But most of these are tolerated because they keep you in a circle of behaviour that the brutes can control. Caffeine keeps you productive. Alcohol dulls you, and if you get violent or make stupid decisions when drunk, they know just how to handle you. But, come off your LSD trip and question the nature of reality, or the motivations behind the economic, moral, or social rules that keep you confined? That, they cannot handle. Maybe sometime in the future, we'll have a world where all people can experience the boundlessness of consciousness and expand behind the contrived reality that they now live in.'

'That's something for me to think about.'

Until now, I had thought about the Boadicea lily as a privileged high—something that Hiroto sought out because of the resources at his disposal. Now, there was some depth to my picture of him—obviously, there was more to him than Sogacorp.

Come dinner time, things were different from the lavish breakfast. We ate a simple meal in the kitchen. Hiroto was nowhere to be seen—from the conversation in the morning I assumed that he was dining separately with his father, and that was an experience that he was not looking forward to.

Post dinner coffee was a fun affair, with Kenji telling me stories which Adachi and Bushida tried to translate. Mrs Fujiwara and Rivkah shared a conspiratorial cigarette at the far end of the patio.

Hiroto emerged about midnight, looking drained and feeble. We drove back to his cottage, drank sake until about three in the morning and then went to bed.

I spent the next day catching up on email and phone calls. Adachi, Bushida, and Hiroto were packing, and there was a steady stream of people coming to the house with bags and packages. Bushida came to me with a well-worn leather backpack and asked me to pack a toothbrush and just one set of clothes. He also gave me a gourd bottle with a belt and asked me to keep it filled.

Chapter 16

At sunrise the next morning, we set out across the meadow. Bushida and Adachi were hauling huge bundles on their backs and Hiroto had a backpack slightly larger than mine. I smelt it again—the inviting earthy fragrance was much stronger now—even more so in the crisp morning air. We walked to a wicker gate that was built into the fence. On the other side, a narrow path led up into the forest. We paused at the gate and Bushida turned to me.

'I want you to remember what Kenji-san told you about the forest.'

I nodded.

'It's deadly serious. It's pulling on you like no one we have ever seen. You will always be within five steps of one of us. If you need to go off for toilet business, one of us will go with you. No matter what you see or hear, you will not leave the path.'

'I understand.'

We started off up the path. The smells of the forest drew me in. We walked slowly—or perhaps the others were pacing themselves by me. The path was dark, and it was hard to tell how high the sun was—barely any sunlight reached the ground. After what felt like an hour, we sat down to rest. My legs were already protesting. The others didn't show any impatience or frustration with this city kid who couldn't walk.

'Thank you for being so kind with me. I know I'm slowing you down,' I said.

'You're not slowing us down,' Hiroto replied. 'We're going to my family's shrine through a forest older than time. This isn't a race, a quest, or a competition. In fact, the more time we take, the better it is. It's a time to reflect and listen to your conscience.' He looked up and around us. 'It's time to open up your mind. Commune with the Kami. We have enough time.'

Something behind me caught his eye. 'Oh, here he comes.'

Coming up the path, was a tall African man—six foot three, perhaps, and muscular—wearing a grey track suit, a red bandana, and carrying a huge bundle on his back. He walked briskly, barely showing exertion. As he neared, Hiroto, Adachi, and Bushida bowed to him. The bundle still on his back, he bowed ever so little in acknowledgement. They exchanged brief comments in Japanese and then he looked at me.

He turned to Adachi, made a curt comment, and marched right on. The three bowed again as he departed.

'Who was that?'

Hiroto looked at me with a smirk on his face. 'The Kannushi. The priest.'

'The priest?' I was incredulous. 'Of your Shinto shrine?'

'Yes.'

'An African priest? Of the Shinto shrine?' I still didn't believe it.

'American,' Adachi said 'Don't be so surprised. If you pass the exam at the university in Ise, you can become a Shinto priest wherever you like.'

'What did he say about me?'

'He told me to keep a close eye on you,' Adachi said. 'He said that the forest is taking you in. The forest spirits will come for you.'

'How does he know?'

'A Kannushi is also a medium. He can speak with the spirits. They speak with him. One of them must have warned him.'

I had a lot to say, but I said nothing. It was as if a world of absurdity lay outside that wooden fence. In his pied-a-terre in Delhi, the Baxter Lodge, or even at his cottage in the Soga compound, Hiroto was at the zenith of reason and rationality. But here, in this forest, everyone suddenly believed in ghosts and spirits and a Shinto priest, who looked like Michael Jai White.

Bushida and Adachi picked their bundles up. We walked on.

About an hour later, we stopped again to rest. The others took off their shoes and socks and flexed their toes. A little white lily caught my eye. White, with little ridges running into the lightest yellow at the centre. I leaned forward to smell it. The baby smell. If you've ever held a day-old child, you'll know what I mean. I heard Srishti giggle. The infant Srishti. The sound I longed for in that empty apartment for two years.

I sniffed the lily again. Guerlain Shalimar.

The scent began to fill me. It seemed as if it was in my blood and vapourising off my skin. I lay in the grass taking in the sensation. I heard Chaaya's voice—distant, barely intelligible. I jumped to my feet. Bushida peered at me with concern on his face.

'Are you alright?'

'Yes. I'm OK.'

They put on their shoes again and we continued walking. I saw something white on a bush beside the path. As we drew closer, I realised what it was—Bunky's napkin. I reached out to grab it, but a gust blew it into a thicket. I dropped my bag and dived in.

I heard Bushida and Adachi shout. Hiroto was screaming my name, telling me to come back. Now if I could just find Bunky's napkin—

'Whatever you saw does not exist!' Hiroto shouted.

'Where are you?'

I didn't say a word.

'What did you see?' came Adachi's voice.

'Bunky's napkin!' I shouted back.

The foliage beside me rustled and Bushida burst through. He grabbed me by the back of my collar and pulled me back to the path.

'That was close,' Hiroto said. 'You're going to have to fight this. If you give in again, we'll have to put a rope around your waist—with a slip knot—and tie the other end to Adachi. Fight it in your head, because your body can't.'

My heart was thumping. Something was wrong.

We walked on.

By late afternoon, we reached a log cabin by the side of the path. It was nearly bare—but was masterfully built—with the kind of workmanship that I had seen in the woodwork in the Soga buildings. In the corner, was a metal wood burning stove with a crockpot inverted on it and a kerosene lantern.

The three of them unpacked. Between Bushida and Adachi, they had nearly everything one needed to live up here. A large bag of rice, small tins of what I thought were condiments, enamel bowls, spoons, towels—the works.

Bushida grabbed an axe that had been hidden in the rafters and asked me to follow him. Hiroto and Adachi picked up slingshots, stuffed their pockets with marbles, and left in another direction. I was famished and thirsty.

Bushida led me to a stream a short distance from the cabin. He filled his bottle from the stream and drank—I did the same. We walked on for a bit and came across a tree with a low-hanging branch. Bushida took off his shirt and got to work cutting it. We dragged it back to the cabin, where he began to chop and stack the wood beside an older pile.

Adachi and Hiroto returned. They had killed perhaps a half dozen small birds. Hiroto took them out to a crude stone table beside the wood stack and cleaned them with a tanto knife. By the time he was done, Adachi had the fire blazing and was cooking rice in the crockpot. Hiroto tossed in the bird meat. Dinner was soup of rice and forest quail. A simple meal flavoured with soy sauce and wasabi—nothing else. But given how tired and hungry I was, it tasted heavenly. I didn't recall another time that I had enjoyed a meal so much.

We slept on the bare wooden floor, with folded towels for pillows. Adachi taught me how to do that right. You fold a standard Turkish bath along the length and then roll it half-way up. You let the roll support your neck and let the rest of the towel keep your head off the floor. It's far more comfortable than any pillow you've ever used—if you sleep flat on your back.

Bushida woke me when it was still dark. Four neatly wrapped cloth bundles lay on the floor. The crockpot was boiling with the previous night's leftovers.

Just as dawn broke, we set out with the bundles on our

backs. After two hours' walk, we passed through a wooden gate in a massive crumbling wall and entered a clearing with four wood and stone buildings. Behind them, a large field of gravestones stood in orderly lines.

Hiroto eyed them with arms akimbo.

'Soga, Kusakabe, Fujiwara, Hashiji, Nakatomi—my ancestors and the men who died beside them in the past eight hundred years.'

He was trembling.

We walked down a simple paved path and reached a little pool fed by a stream. The three of them stripped naked and walked in chin-deep. Bushida beckoned—I understood I had to follow suit. I undressed, self-conscious about my flabby city body—so different from these three toned murder machines.

The water was ice cold, but refreshing. It washed off my aches and pains, and left me feeling alert and vigorous.

We stepped out of the water and opened the cloth bundles. Mine held a towel, some clothes I didn't really understand, and a pair of straw slippers. I dried myself, and Adachi helped me dress—in a loin cloth, in elaborate folds of a cream kimono and a dark blue sash.

Once dressed in our kimonos, we folded our walking clothes into neat bundles by the pool and returned up the path.

We left our slippers outside the largest of the four buildings and entered. The Kannushi stood there—dressed in a purple kimono and scarlet cap. Bushida, Adachi, and Hiroto bowed to him. A well-rehearsed exchange followed between them. Adachi, Bushida, and I sat on straw mats, while the priest and Hiroto entered one of the inner rooms.

I smelled incense and heard the sound of chanting. It must have lasted an hour.

When they returned, Bushida and Adachi stood up and bowed to Hiroto. The three picked up bundles of incense from a nearby table and walked into the graveyard.

For two hours, I watched them move from grave to grave, lighting incense, and praying. Once they were done, Hiroto took me for a walk among the graves. He pointed out the names of his ancestors going back centuries—other graves too—remarkable people who had been associated with the clan over the centuries.

We returned to one of the smaller buildings in the temple complex. The priest led us into one of the rooms that appeared to be set up for some sort of ceremony. The floor was covered with tatami mats—a low table was in the centre with two cups and a porcelain bottle.

Bushida, Adachi, and the priest sat at the edges of the room. Hiroto directed me to the table. I sat there across from him.

'I'm sure you now understand that Sogacorp is not a regular investment fund,' Hiroto said to me.

'That's been obvious for a while.'

'With the acquisition of Linguintel, I'm giving you

a chance to be a part of this. A part of Sogacorp in the true sense. For as long as you choose to remain associated, you will be a part of the Soga Han. You, your family, and everyone close to you will be cared for by Sogacorp. No matter what happens.'

'That sounds a bit arrogant. Why is this necessary?' I asked.

'Continuity,' Hiroto said. 'Do you see the privilege we have? The graves that I showed you go back eight hundred years. Three families have stayed together—building, rebuilding, celebrating, mourning. This is what we achieved. Even when reduced to almost nothing, we bounced back bigger than ever in seventy years. Commit to Sogacorp. Build with us.'

'I wish I had time to think about this.'

Hiroto smiled. 'I'm sorry to spring this on you. I made up my mind about this only last night. We're on sacred ground, and it means a lot that we do this here.' He pointed to the side, 'think in solitude for a bit. You don't have to do this, and you certainly don't have to do this today.'

Adachi rose and opened a sliding door.

I stood up and walked into an empty room with just the traditional mats on the floor.

I paced for a bit. Then sat down to think. My mind was a whirlwind—things were moving just too fast for me.

I was confused. I wasn't sure what I was getting myself into. The past couple of weeks had been quite an experience—living and working with Hiroto and his inner circle. He was certainly someone I wanted to be associated with. Unlike Akshay Bhalla, Hiroto's warmth and openness was unique. Then it struck me—he was trying to play the part of a benevolent Japanese chieftain in the twenty-first century. That's what travelling the world with two male companions was all about. The Daimyo and his bodyguards. It was working for him though. He enjoyed the devotion of pretty much everyone who came into contact with him. I liked him too.

And this place—it felt so welcoming. Even though it had been my first time visiting—not just at the Soga Compound, but the country—I felt a call, a sense of belonging. Of course—maybe it was just my heart grasping at the first time I felt understood and appreciated in so many years—Chaaya and her link to Hiroto and Sogacorp. But it was real. Hiroto was putting his money where his mouth was.

My mind was made up.

I returned to the table.

'I will commit to Sogacorp,' I said my voice trembling slightly. 'What do I have to do?'

'A Covenant,' Hiroto said. 'I, as the head of Sogacorp, am committing to you, your family, and your connections. You, as a part of Sogacorp, are committing to Sogacorp and my goals.'

'I agree.'

Hiroto poured me half a cup of sake and poured himself a full cup. 'Drink.'

We drank.

He refilled both cups to the brim and switched them. 'Drink.'

We drank.

'Now, the priest will enter your name in the Sogacorp register.'

The priest said something in Japanese.

'Your children too,' Hiroto added, 'whether you're married to their mother or not.'

The priest led us to another room, where a large book was open to a blank page. He looked at my name written in the Roman alphabet on a scrap of paper, and then wrote in Japanese script in the book. I wrote out Srishti's name on that scrap; he looked at it and added some more lines. When he was done, Hiroto stamped the page twice with a small round seal.

We returned to the cabin that afternoon. Hiroto and Adachi went hunting again. Bushida taught me his wood chopping technique. Chopping wood felt great. I was intoxicated by the swing of the heavy axe and the crunch with which it made contact with the wood. I may have overdone it. My hands had terrible blisters. My shoulders and stomach hurt like hell. Once we were done chopping the wood, Bushida taught me how to sharpen the axe—rubbing gently in slow circles on a smooth rock until it could shave the hair on the back of my hand.

Hiroto and Adachi returned with rabbits. We ate rabbit and rice stew around an outdoor fire. After we finished and washed our plates, we sat around the embers in silence. Hiroto and I smoked American Spirit cigarettes.

A gust of wind hit him in the face and he turned to me.

'Reason and rationality are illusions that we have created to frame our perceptions in the material world,' he said. 'It's very easy to explain what you can, and shrug at what you can't—perhaps stuffing it in the closet of unknown things. Think about it—even the boffins at CERN—with the most advanced equipment are unable to understand how atoms actually work—to the point that every couple of years they come up with a new particle that explains a bump in some graph somewhere. We never know anything. We have lived here for a thousand years. Our lives, history, destinies are tied to this forest and everything in it. It's not superstition—it's experience and tradition. If you live with your mind open, every moment will show you something that science struggles to explain.'

'That's what's happened to me since I saw the forest,' I said. 'So many things that I can't explain.'

'Do you know what people will say if you tell them about it? Oh, you're imagining it. Were you high? You must be delusional. Anything outside of a narrow and contrived reality is considered absurd or insanity.'

We did not have a cell phone signal in the forest, and

my anxiety from being disconnected had begun to fade. Hiroto didn't seem too rushed about returning. We rose at dawn, bathed in the stream, did laundry on the rocks, and ate small game that Hiroto, Bushida, and Adachi brought back from the forest. I got addicted to chopping wood. My next favourite pastime was sharpening the axe on a stone beside the cabin that had a lot of wear on it. Bushida told me that his uncle had taught him to sharpen an axe on that very stone when he was a boy. Hiroto recounted a childhood memory of Kenji using it when he was up here hunting with a group of male relatives.

There's an inexplainable joy in being idle—no Facebook feed to scroll, no WhatsApp messages to read or respond to. I was here in the forest—with the sounds of birds and the wind—and these three men, who were now my clan. The true significance of my joining Sogacorp began to sink in. I was adding myself to a history. At meals and in idle time, Hiroto, Bushida, and Adachi told me stories. These stories were a mix of legend, genealogy, and history.

I dreamt at night. They were inscrutable, technicolour dreams that I couldn't make much of. It felt as if I was looking at the world from the bottom of a crystal-clear pool. I remembered Kenji telling me about the Kami, and maybe this is how it worked. They don't walk up to you to tell you anything. They draw you in—these muffled voices—the smell of the forest—lilies that smell of Shalimar, Bunky's napkin—all props to pull you into a space that seems real, but isn't. Something of a bent reality. But isn't that true of all dreams?

One night, I awoke abruptly from such a dream. The door of the cabin was wide open, and the forest, curiously, was absolutely silent. The other three were fast asleep. The wind brought me a whisper. The moonlight coloured the ground silver—were it not for the comfortable forest breeze smelling of wood and moss, you would think it was snow. I sensed danger. Bushida always locked the door when we turned in—a ceramic and copper chime above it would sound every time it was opened. Obviously, this moment was for me. *Fight it in your head*—Hiroto had said. Was this real, or am I in my head?

'You built it,' the wind whispered to me in Puran's voice. 'Linguistic Intelligence.'

I stepped out of the cabin. The wind died down and the forest went completely silent. Then I saw him. Seated on a fallen tree, wearing his cream coloured night suit.

'Hi Harish.'

I didn't know how to respond. It was a voice that I hadn't heard for a very long time. Of course this wasn't real. I walked up and sat beside him.

'So, you built it. Linguistic Intelligence. And you found him. What took you so long?'

'Life happened Puran. Life. The world is such a difficult place to be in. I'm sure you see it; it takes everything just to survive.'

'And yet, you get to live, eat good food, drink good booze, sleep with beautiful women—and I'm stuck here.'

'What do you want me to do?' I asked. 'What can I do? I wish you hadn't killed yourself. I miss you every day, and I've never had a friend like you.'

'You've found who did it. What are you going to do?'

'I don't know. I don't think there is much I can do. It is more than twenty years since you died. I don't even think that the authorities will reopen the case. Also, Linguintel is a tool. It will take a lot of work to even convince a court that it is evidence.'

'Jaydip confessed,' Puran hissed. 'He confessed to you. What are you going to do?'

My hair stood on end and my heart started thumping. This did not sound like Puran at all. He pulled out a packet of Panama unfiltered cigarettes and lit one.

'You're not Puran!' I shouted, jumping away.

'Do you think we stay the same?' he howled—his voice echoed through the trees.

He floated to me, brought his face close to mine and blinked. His eyes started glowing green. His teeth were brown and pointed. 'You're one of them. You enjoyed the *Adventures of Puran* too. Secretly. You found them funny. You're as guilty as Jaydip.'

'That is not true.' I was frantic. 'You were the best friend I ever had. You knew what it was like to be mocked your entire life for being bookish, or too smart. The one who couldn't fight or catch a cricket ball. You were the one person in my entire life who knew what it was like to be me!'

'Do you know what it feels like to die like I did?' He grabbed my throat and his fingers seemed to lengthen until he had a grip around my neck.

'You are not Puran. You can't be.'

His hand turned into a coarse coir noose. I felt a painful tug and we went flying up into the trees. It hurt. My head was becoming heavy, my eyes felt as if they would pop out of their sockets. I was choking, hanging about ten feet above the ground with the Kami somewhere above me. The world was going dark.

As my vision tunnelled, I saw the Kannushi, dressed in his full ceremonial garb, come sprinting through the trees to where I was hanging. When he reached me, he jumped like a basketball player on lay-up and wound a white cord around my ankle.

The noose released and I lost consciousness.

I woke up on the floor of the cabin in broad daylight. The Kannushi was sitting beside me. My neck was bandaged, and the white cord, with a little red pouch on it, was wound tight around my right wrist.

'Wear this until you leave the forest,' the Kannushi said to me in American accented English. 'If you take it off while you're in the forest, you will die.'

Hiroto, Bushida, and Adachi sat on the floor against

the far wall of the cabin. All three looked sulky.

'This is nobody's fault,' the Kannushi said in a commanding tone. 'I need you to keep your minds clear. This is how Kami begin their attacks on mortals. Purge any guilt and rumination. Do not leave the forest unless you're at peace, or you will take the Kami with you.'

Hiroto muttered something in Japanese and the Kannushi glowered at him.

'Why is my friend suffering?' I asked the Kannushi.

'He's not your friend. Souls are complex forces. You know on Earth, our upbringing, training, society—they give us certain habits and personalities. But in a very fundamental sense, we are composed of an infinite evil and an infinite good. Most of humanity lives close to the very fine centre line. The spirit world has no impositions for souls to behave themselves.'

'He's suffering. He's envious.'

'And that has nothing to do with you. We can recite from the Lotus Sutra for him, but there is nothing that you can do in the real world that will bring him peace. Angry spirits demand outrageous things—do not be tempted to interfere.'

I tried to get up but felt a sharp pain in my lower back.

'Stay still,' the Kannushi said. 'You had quite a serious fall and your back may be hurt. You'll rest here for a few days until you can return.'

'Can we recite from the Lotus Sutra?'

'If you can walk to the temple tomorrow morning, we will start.'

Bushida woke me before dawn and escorted me to the temple where we found the Kannushi waiting. I bathed in the pool and dressed in my kimono. I sat in the main temple building with my eyes closed, while the Kannushi burned incense and chanted from memory. The incense and chanting were hypnotic. I found myself sliding down rabbit holes of thought—memories, ruminations, what if, and so forth. It was terrible. I kept reminding myself that I was here for Puran, not for myself. But then, when one is so preoccupied by the weight of his own life, how does he do anything for anyone else?

As the incense burned, I began to feel patches in my body—shame, guilt, disgust, sadness.

At the end of it all I felt heavier, burdened by an invisible weight and lacking meaning or purpose.

On the second day, this heaviness started to lift. I began to wonder what the Kannushi was chanting. He seemed to recite from memory, but did have a book before him. I decided to just stay in the moment. It was hard to begin with, but as time passed, I was able to sustain longer periods of clarity. The practice of '*presence*' that started on that lonely hilltop in Baxterpur was finally taking hold.

On the third day, I made it a point to focus on Puran. I tried to recall his face, his voice, specific incidents. Is it just me, or is this hard to do when you want to do it with intention? I remember being haunted by him in the nights after his death.

Haunted by him? Those were my thoughts, my guilt. Letting go was for me.

The Kannushi stopped chanting abruptly.

'We're done.'

The next day, we trekked back to the Soga compound.

Chapter 17

At the Soga compound we caught up with the news on Shaybee and Akshay Bhalla. It seemed that the attack had upped the pace of everything. Merrill Lynch and Blackrock, announced their own investigations into their dealings with Shaybee and an 'exhaustive review of their sub-fund selection processes' or some such. The narrative on the attack had changed. One of the surviving attackers had told the police that the attack was a contract hit.

Akshay Bhalla was a wanted man.

We returned to India to close the Linguintel transaction. Harry, Chaaya, and a team of lawyers and bankers had been camping at the Imperial Hotel in Delhi. After three days of some pretty intense back and forth, Linguintel belonged to Sogacorp.

GK and I drove up to Baxterpur. Hiroto and his entourage flew up. We gathered for a celebratory dinner on the Baxter Lodge's terrace. It wasn't a party by any measure. The lodge's kitchen staff set up a live grill and we drank Sudo Honke.

I introduced GK to Hiroto as the man who would guide his vision for Linguintel.

'You'll have to tell me his vision first,' GK scoffed. Incorrigible. I had told him perhaps a dozen times during the drive to dial down his impudence.

'Ah! Come over here.' Hiroto pointed to the seat at the head of the table. 'I love talking about my vision. Pour him a drink.'

Harry poured GK a cup of sake and Hiroto launched into his speech with the Sogashoes parable.

When he began to explain what he wanted to do with Linguintel, GK's lips began to twitch—never a good sign. When Hiroto gave the example of selling a Toyota Corolla to Puff Daddy, GK bellowed with laughter. 'This makes you Shaybee Part 2,' he cackled.

Hiroto was stunned. 'Why would you say that?'

GK emptied his sake cup and put it back on the table.

'See, this whole social media nonsense—there's no money or use in it. Your plan is just adding masala to the jingbang. Do you have any idea how powerful the linguistic engine is? This is a waste of the engine. Just like all iPhone users wasting their supercomputer watching bikini babes in Instagram all the time.'

I looked around the table. Surprisingly, nobody seemed annoyed. Harry refilled GK's cup.

'If you want to do something big with Linguintel, use it for medical research.' He punctuated his speech with a sip.

'The whole world knows only the English language medical research. However, so many of the researches are done in other languages. The Ayurveda writings are in Sanskrit, Tamil, Telugu, Malayalam. Unani in Urdu and Persian. African tropical diseases info is in French, Portuguese and that South Africa language. South America has so much information in Spanish and Portuguese. And then in Europe—Czech, Polish, Hungarian. The Russians during USSR time did more research than all English language countries. We do not even know how much Chinese medical research is there. Put the Linguistic engine on the research. Train the model and feed the research. Use OCR scanning for the paper documents, indexing and all will happen in a computing cluster, and give the open source feed for all medical institutions to use whatever research in whatever language they want. It will be a real game changer for the entire planet.

Hiroto's jaw dropped.

Harry turned to Hiroto. 'Time for another shopping trip?'

'How the fuck do you know all this?' I asked GK.

'I did research, guru. Shaybee was always looking for something to do with the product. I have made seven business plans in last three years but they did not see the potential. If this guy is such a charity maharaja wanting to change the world and all that jazz, this is best plan for him.'

'Send me the other six business plans too—will you, GK?' said Harry.

'Done sir.'

'Wait. Wait,' Hiroto interjected, 'this conversation is not over. I have questions.'

Hiroto, Harry, and GK drew into a huddle at the end of the table and Bushida walked up with a fresh bottle of sake.

'Look at this boss!' GK bellowed, holding up the bottle. 'Our business discussions have gone from Old Monk Rum to Bhalla's Scotch Whiskey to this Japanese booze.'

Chaaya, Adachi, and I sat down to dinner. Ever so often I looked over to where GK in his typical boisterous style was speaking to Hiroto and Harry. They listened enraptured. About 2 am, Chaaya and I left. We showered and changed for bed, and she fell asleep immediately.

I felt rage—perhaps envy. Linguintel had been mine, and now GK was eclipsing me. I stayed awake all night wondering what my place in Linguintel would be going forward. GK had seven business plans. He's a smart guy—think about it—he rose from being a waiter at a dive bar with a computer skills course, to being the technical lead of a cutting-edge startup. The more I thought about it, the less threatened I felt. At worst, in a year or so, Hiroto would fire me with a golden handshake and I could go find something else to do. That's easy in a place like Delhi. When you're a startup founder with two successful exits, it's quite easy to find something new to do. Also, I have money.

The next morning, GK joined Chaaya and me for breakfast at the lobby cafe. When we were halfway through, Bushida walked up and asked us to come to Suite 23 when we were done.

Suite 23 was bare. Carpets covered the floor and a small table sat in the centre of the room, with two cups and a bottle of sake on it. I realised that this was the covenant ceremony that I had gone through at the Soga temple a few days earlier.

Hiroto, Bushida, Adachi, and Harry entered from a side door, dressed in black suits. Hiroto sat by the table, and the others sat on the floor along the far wall of the room. Bushida motioned to GK, and he reluctantly joined Hiroto at the table. He kept looking over his shoulder at me, seeking an explanation.

'OK, what?' he asked Hiroto.

'GK, Sogacorp is more than just a company.'

'I know,' GK said.

When I heard his tone, I was sure that this meeting would rapidly turn sour. I was just hoping that it didn't escalate into a fistfight, because GK can brawl.

Hiroto paused, peering at GK—perhaps trying to gauge what would happen next. 'I am giving you a chance to take a larger part in the future of Linguintel and of Sogacorp.'

'How?'

'A covenant,' Hiroto said. 'I, as the head of Sogacorp, am committing to you, your family, and your connections. You, as a part of Sogacorp, are committing to Sogacorp and my goals.'

GK looked back at me. 'What does commendant mean boss?'

'Covenant. A promise,' I replied.

'OK. Big word for this Japanese mafia ceremony.'

'What?' I almost shouted. 'GK, I know you like to be the joker all the time, but there are some times in life that you must be serious.'

'Why now boss? These guys all in fancy dress are making me to make mafia promise?'

Harry sniggered and then pinched his nose in an effort to contain his laughter. Hiroto's eyes were glassy—it took all of his Japanese stoicism and English restraint not to react. Bushida and Adachi were stone-faced but their cheeks were colouring rapidly—from mirth or from anger—it was hard to tell.

Harry came up to the table and knelt beside GK. 'Look, I don't think this is going the way anyone expected it to.' He placed his hand on GK's shoulder. 'You're right. This ceremony—the sake promise—*is* used by the Yakuza—and that's perhaps how you have seen it in movies. But this is actually an ancient tradition—a way to seal a promise. It's used at weddings, in politics, in diplomacy, in business, even among siblings—whenever a serious promise needs to be made.'

'But what Mr Soga said does not sound like a promise. It sounds like me bowing to him.'

'Well…' Harry paused—looking for words. 'I can see why you think that.'

'Not interested,' GK said. 'For me there is only two people I will bow my head. One is Lord Balaji and the other is Mr Harish Arya.'

A tense silence followed.

'I respect that,' Hiroto said. He tipped over the sake cups, spilling their contents onto the table. He stood up and barged out of the room followed by Bushida and Adachi.

'Are we in trouble?' I asked Harry.

'I think we will have to chop off our finger in the evening,' GK quipped.

'Oh no, no GK,' Harry waved dismissively.

'Things will just go on the way they were. Toto isn't one to carry a grudge. Also, he's terribly fond of you both.'

He paused thoughtfully for a second.

'Just stop the Yakuza jibes, ok? Even someone as refined as Toto can run out of patience, and I personally can never understand what's going on with Bushida, Adachi, or Kenji.'

That evening, I went to the western gazebo to relax. The century-old wrought iron bench was filled with a sense of warmth. I wondered about who had sat here. Just a few months ago, I remember I had been here, simmering in my crush on Chaaya, sipping the scotch that Dr Bhatnagar prescribed. Anupama had been here—perhaps she had a premonition of things to come—hence her words to Chaaya that inspired the memento for her grandfather.

Hiroto sat beside me. I felt the need to apologise.

'I'm sorry about GK's behaviour,' I said softly, 'I literally picked him off the street, so he's an absolute boor.'

'He's not boorish—he's loyal.'

'That he is,' I acknowledged.

'You know, at some point about twelve hundred years ago, two ambitious samurai—a Soga and a Nakatomi pledged brotherhood. Today, three samurai bloodlines with a total of fifteen thousand known descendants are a part of this story. My point is that you have the opportunity to build something great. It always starts with two people who are loyal and unflinching.'

I processed this in silence for a few moments.

'Let's go for a walk,' he said.

We grabbed our cameras and sauntered down to the camera shop.

Bhikshu Dechen was delighted. He took our cameras and wiped down the lenses. I handed him the roll from mine to be sent in for processing. The table in the corner had just—one stool and two coarse wooden benches—dinner was a real squeeze.

The prints came back in a few days. Two of them really jumped out at me. The one that I took of Srishti was beautiful. The way the Canon lens captured natural light was exquisite. The wall behind her had a narrow strip of stained-glass tiles, and the camera had caught my reflection in them. It looked as if I was kneeling just behind her as she played with Bunky and a toy car.

The second was of the men in the silver van. I recognised the driver—the man in the orange shirt, who burst in first through the door during the house attack. The driver's window was partly lowered—and the glare on the glass obscured his right hand. It made it seem as if his hand was severed at the wrist. The person behind him had his window up all the way, but the reflection of something nearby—foliage perhaps—made it look as if half his face was missing. I recalled from the news reports that they had taken two days to identify one of the men because of his injuries.

I shuffled through the images and got to the one of us dining in Nara. Just a regular picture—blurry—of four guys sitting down for a meal.

So, did the dream lens really see the future? Perhaps, but I don't think it empowered us to change anything.

Chapter 18

A few days later, Hiroto, Adachi, Bushida, and I dropped in at Dwidala Camera Shop while walking around town. Bhikshu Dechen knocked on the shutter. The boy walked in, straining under a stack of four trays—a truly epic balancing act.

Right at the top was a porcelain bowl—one of those seen in homes all over India. Cream coloured with a gold rim, and pale pink flowers. An off-white plastic plate covered it with a silver teaspoon on it. Bhikshu Dechen lifted it off the top and gently set it down on the counter. The boy unloaded the tray at the table and left.

We were halfway through the meal when Akshay Bhalla barged into the shop.

'You've taken everything! Everything's gone. Finished!' he howled. 'Everything that I worked for. Everything that ever gave me joy!' He pulled out a silver revolver.

'No—' said Bhikshu Dechen, wagging his finger at Adachi and Bushida.

They froze—seemingly unable to move anything but their eyes. He stood up. It may have been his robes billowing in the draught or that he's a large man, but as he stood there, Bhalla couldn't take a shot.

'Out of my way!' Bhalla shrieked. 'Out of my way now, or I'm going to shoot you too.'

'With what?' Bhikshu Dechen asked.

He turned around and returned to his seat at the table.

Bhalla stared at his empty hand in astonishment. His index finger curled around a trigger that wasn't there. He stood there transfixed for perhaps ten seconds—then he saw the porcelain bowl.

He went over to it—his entire body trembling.

He picked up the spoon and examined it. 'Where did you…' he put the plate aside and burst into tears. 'Where did this come from?'

He picked up the bowl and sat on the ground. 'My naani's phirni.' He took a taste and started sobbing.

Footsteps sounded outside and a group of men ran to the door of the shop. The monk rolled his eyes and stood up.

'*Iddhar hai*!' someone shouted.

A man came into the shop. 'Delhi Police. He prodded Bhalla with his foot. 'Where is the gun?'

'My naani's phirni,' said Bhalla, without even looking up from the bowl.

The man's voice got sterner, 'Where is the gun!' he shouted—drawing back for a kick.

'What gun?' the monk asked, stuffing himself between the cop and Bhalla.

The man leaned ferociously towards Bhikshu Dechen. 'When he left Brodie House, he had a gun. Where is the gun?'

The monk didn't even blink. 'When you left Himalay Lodge you had a gun,' the monk said. 'Where is your gun?'

The man's eyes widened. He pulled back his jacket to reveal an empty under-arm holster.

'*Abbey! Meri pistol kidhar gayi*?'

He stumbled backwards out of the shop shouting to the others in Hindi. From their frantic conversation, it sounded as if three other service pistols had disappeared.

Bhikshu Dechen sat on the floor and put his arm around Bhalla.

Acknowledgements

This book would never have seen the light of day without the constant encouragement and support from Ashutosh Thakur. Atul Thakur connected me to the brilliant folks at Vitasta who made this book happen. This book would never have been completed if it wasn't for the feedback and support from my wife Varsha Sindhu. Thanks also to Prashant Mahagaonkar, Tanushree Bhasin, and Deepanshu Tyagi for reading through the first draft and giving me actionable feedback. Artdwara, run by Shashank Verma, gave me a quiet and creatively fertile space to complete the first draft of this book.

I'm deeply grateful to you all.